E.P. JACOBS

ATLANTIS MYSTERY

9th CINEBOOK
The 9th Art Publisher

Original title: L'énigme de l'Atlantide

Original edition: © Editions Blake & Mortimer / Studio Jacobs (Dargaud – Lombard S.A.) 1988
by E.P. Jacobs
www.dargaud.com
All rights reserved

English translation: © 2011 Cinebook Ltd

Translator: Jerome Saincantin
Lettering and text layout: Imadjinn
Printed in Spain by Just Colour Graphic

This edition first published in Great Britain in 2012 by
Cinebook Ltd
56 Beech Avenue
Canterbury, Kent
CT4 7TA
www.cinebook.com

A CIP catalogue record for this book
is available from the British Library

ISBN 978-1-84918-107-5

PROFESSOR PHILIP MORTIMER HAS COME TO THE ENCHANTING ISLAND OF SAO MIGUEL TO SPEND A FEW WEEKS' HOLIDAY. ITS STRANGE AND MAGNIFICENT SITES, COMBINED WITH A PAST SHROUDED IN MYSTERY, MAKE THE "GREEN ISLAND" THE MOST RENOWNED PART OF THE AZORES. AN EXTREMELY ANCIENT TRADITION HOLDS THAT IT IS ONE OF THE EMERGED SUMMITS OF ATLANTIS, THAT MYSTERIOUS LOST CONTINENT DESCRIBED BY THE PHILOSOPHER PLATO, WHICH, IN A MYSTICAL PAST, IS SUPPOSED TO HAVE VANISHED INTO THE DEPTHS OF THE ATLANTIC OCEAN...

IT WAS ENOUGH FOR THE PROFESSOR, EVER EAGER FOR NEW AND UNEXPECTED ADVENTURES, TO BEGIN EXPLORING THE WILD VALES AND CANYONS NEAR THE VOLCANIC VALLEY OF FURNAS. IT LED HIM TO A SURPRISING DISCOVERY—SO SURPRISING, IN FACT, THAT HE IMMEDIATELY CONTACTED HIS OLD FRIEND, CAPTAIN FRANCIS BLAKE. AS THIS EXTRAORDINARY STORY BEGINS, MORTIMER IS AT THE SANT' ANA AIRFIELD TO WELCOME THE CAPTAIN. BUT NO SOONER HAVE OUR TWO FRIENDS LEFT THE TERMINAL, ALREADY DEEP IN A LIVELY DISCUSSION, THAN THE PLOT BEGINS TO THICKEN!...

FROM BEHIND A GLASS PANE, A MAN OBSERVES THE TRAVELLERS' EXIT...

There they are!!...

IMMEDIATELY, THE STRANGER GIVES A WHISTLE. TWO OTHER MEN, BENT OVER AN OLD FORD SOME DISTANCE AWAY, RECOGNISE THE SOUND AS A SIGNAL.

FWEEET

Look out!

It's done!...

WHILE LEADING BLAKE TOWARDS HIS CAR, MORTIMER EXCLAIMS:

I'm simply flabbergasted by what you just told me! Someone stole the letter in which I informed you of my discovery?!... But how could anyone have known?...

I asked myself the same question. And, considering its content, I took the liberty of involving the I.S.*...

You did the right thing! But here's the car. Get in; we'll be at my place in a jiffy.

Jolly good! I'm eager to see the thing up close. I must confess I'm rather uneasy about it...

How far is it to Furnas?

A good 45 minutes...

BUT, AS THE CAR STARTS, THE MAN WHO'D BEEN WATCHING FOR BLAKE'S ARRIVAL SNIGGERS...

Have a nice walk, gentlemen!

THE CAR PULLS INTO THE MAIN ROAD AND SPEEDS AWAY. BUT SOON...

Let's turn off here. It's quicker, and there's less traffic...

THE CONVERSATION CONTINUES AS THEY DRIVE...

I don't need to tell you that I did everything in my power to keep the subject of my investigations secret. Should my hypothesis turn out to be true, the consequences of my find could be devastating, depending on how it is used!...

Yes. That is precisely what worries me about the theft: Only a powerful organisation or a spy ring would show any interest in such thing. And in that case, it's going to be...

BUT A RATTLING AND COUGHING FROM THE ENGINE INTERRUPTS THE CAPTAIN...

Oh, what now? That ruddy engine again! Never a moment's peace with these rented vehicles!...

PRT PTT RTT

THE CAR GOES ANOTHER FEW YARDS, THEN STOPS ALTOGETHER...

Nothing too serious, I hope?...

I hope so, too, because this road isn't very busy... and night falls quickly here...

*INTELLIGENCE SERVICE (BRITISH INTELLIGENCE)

LIFTING THE BONNET, MORTIMER CONDUCTS A QUICK INSPECTION...

The ignition?...

More than likely. Let's see...

...AND SUDDENLY...

By George! Sugar! Sugar in the petrol! Look at this sparking plug...

Sugar?! So, it was sabotage?...

...QUICKLY, THE TWO MEN CONFER...

I was expected—that much is obvious! And I'd lay a thousand-to-one odds that someone wanted to keep us away from your place.

That must be it! No sense in hanging around here then. Let's walk back to the main road, and then... trust in Providence.

MEANWHILE, HOWEVER, IN THE ALREADY DARK GROUNDS OF "QUINTA DO PICO", MORTIMER'S RESIDENCE, A DRAMATIC EVENT HAS JUST TAKEN PLACE...

There! I shouldn't be disturbed for a good while.

APPARENTLY SATISFIED, THE MASKED STRANGER QUICKLY MAKES HIS WAY ACROSS THE LAWN AND UP A FEW STEPS, PUSHES OPEN A FRENCH WINDOW AND ENTERS THE SILENT VILLA...

Perfect! And now, to work...

TAKING OUT A SMALL, OBLONG BOX FROM UNDER HIS CLOAK, HE SNIGGERS.

With this, it'll be child's play.

THEN, ADVANCING SLOWLY, STEP BY STEP, THE MAN BEGINS SWEEPING HIS PECULIAR DEVICE ALL AROUND HIM...

AFTER HAVING METHODICALLY GONE OVER THE GROUND FLOOR, THE VILLAIN GOES UP A STAIRCASE...

Let's see up there now...

THERE, GOING FROM ROOM TO ROOM, HE INSPECTS THAT STOREY AND IS BEGINNING TO LOSE PATIENCE. WHEN, SUDDENLY, AS HE PUSHES ONE LAST DOOR, THE DEVICE EMITS A STRANGE LITTLE SOUND...

At last!

BOP BOP BOP

HAVING PERFORMED A FEW PRUDENT SWEEPS, THE STRANGER FINALLY LOCATES THE PLACE HE HAS SO ARDENTLY SOUGHT...

Careful now! It's here, in this corner... But...

BOP BOP BOP

What? In this aquarium?... Good old Professor! As cunning as ever!

BOP BOP BOP

WITHOUT HESITATION, HE PLUNGES HIS HAND INTO THE WATER AND FEVERISHLY CLAWS THROUGH THE SAND AND ROCKS THAT COVER THE BOTTOM.

ALL AT ONCE, HE EXCLAIMS TRIUMPHANTLY...

I've got it!!

BUT, AT THAT MOMENT, SOFT LAUGHTER MAKES HIM LOSE HIS GRIP.

Ha! Ha! Ha!

STRUCK DUMB WITH SURPRISE, HE SEES A STRANGE SILHOUETTE FRAMED INSIDE THE DOOR.

WITH A SHOUT OF RAGE, THE MASKED MAN GOES FOR HIS PISTOL, BUT...

Oh!...

...THE NEWLY-ARRIVED STRANGER RAISES HIS ARM. WITH A DRY CRACKLING, A BLINDING RAY OF LIGHT STRIKES THE BURGLAR, WHO FALLS OVER BACKWARD...

Ow!!!

AT THE SAME MOMENT, A TRUCK THAT HAD BEEN APPROACHING AT TOP SPEED STOPS IN FRONT OF THE GARDEN GATE IN A GREAT SQUEAL OF BRAKES...

EEEEEE

MORTIMER AND BLAKE CLIMB OUT HURRIEDLY.

Please accept this, and thank you for your help...

Era um prazer, senhor*!

Hurry up, old chap!

PUSHING PAST THE GATE, THE TWO MEN WALK BRISKLY INTO THE GARDEN.

That truck was a godsend. Without it, we'd still be trudging along that...

Shhh!... Listen!...

A LOW MOANING CAN BE HEARD COMING FROM A NEARBY BUSH...

Heavens!

There, look! A man on the ground!

*IT WAS A PLEASURE, SIR.

IN AN INSTANT, THEY'RE KNEELING BY THE WOUNDED MAN...

Blimey! It's Zarco, my manservant! The poor man was knocked out.

Did we get here too late, then!?

INSTINCTIVELY, BLAKE TURNS AROUND TO LOOK TOWARDS THE VILLA AND LETS OUT A STARTLED CRY...

Philip!

?

A MAN HAS JUST LANDED ON THE TERRACE AFTER JUMPING OUT A WINDOW ONE STOREY UP...

WITHOUT A WORD, OUR TWO FRIENDS HAVE LEAPT FORWARD...

He disappeared behind the house!

Good! There's no other way out of there. The terrace is surrounded by a ravine 100 feet deep!

BUT, JUST AS THEY ARE ABOUT TO ARRIVE, THEY'RE STOPPED IN THEIR TRACKS BY AN INCREDIBLE SIGHT: WITH A LOW WHISTLING SOUND, A STRANGE MACHINE COMES OUT OF A BUSH, ZOOMS THROUGH THE AIR AT LIGHTNING SPEED, AND VANISHES!!

! !

Francis, old boy!... Did you see that... that thing?!

Yes!... I think we can stop the chase here...

3

PECULIAR BURGLARY AT THE QUINTA DO PICO

"Yes, someone knocked out my servant and broke into my home," declares the current tenant of the villa, Pr. Mortimer, to the detective in charge of the investigation...

Yesterday towards 8:30 p.m., as he was making his usual round before closing the gate, Zarco Nèves, servant at the Quinta do Pico, rented some time ago by Professor Mortimer, was knocked out in the garden by an unseen attacker. Shortly afterwards, after being delayed by an automobile breakdown on his way back from the Sant' Ana airfield, where he'd gone to pick up a friend, the professor found the unfortunate servant lying behind a bush...

WHAT WAS THE BURGLAR LOOKING FOR?

However, while the terse statement the professor gave the police seems to have satisfied the officer in charge of the case, Inspector Henriques, it does not appear to have convinced everyone. Certain reporters speak of rumours going around Furnas, concerning certain trips the professor took around the wild canyons and forests near Povoação. Trips that ... seems reluctant to

MORE FLYING SAUCERS?...

Last night, around 9 p.m., an inhabitant ... maintains

IN A ROOM AT THE CENTRAL HOTEL IN PONTE DELGADO, TWO MEN ARE HAVING A SOMEWHAT SOUR EXCHANGE...

Fine, let's just forget about it!...

Believe me, Colonel. You'd be better off dropping your fantastic account of last night's events!... You can see that the newspapers don't...

THE MAN ADDRESSED AS COLONEL WHIRLS AROUND, HIS FACE TWISTED WITH RAGE, AND WE CAN NOW RECOGNISE HIM... OLRIK, THE ELUSIVE ADVENTURER AND ETERNAL OPPONENT OF BLAKE AND MORTIMER!

By thunder!... I told you before... That devilish weapon was no ordinary piece... Lightning shot out of it, and bam!... It was like a sledgehammer blow to my guts!!! By the time I came to, the other guy had vanished with the loot... I heard shouts in the garden and barely had time to run. My legs were shaky and my skull was still ringing like a bell!...

Listen, my dear fellow, if my government turned to you to get your hands on that... thing, it wasn't to hear you justify your failures with wild stories!... An unknown weapon? Ha, ha! Don't make me laugh! Was it used by some Martian fresh off last night's flying saucer, maybe?!...

All right, Ostrog, cut the sarcasm!... I'll get my revenge!...

AT THAT MOMENT, AT THE QUINTA DO PICO, MORALE ISN'T ANY BETTER!

I could have done without this publicity! And to think we were just discussing the need for discretion!

Ah! Let's just be thankful that no one had the idea of linking our story to that of the flying object!!...

Wouldn't that be dandy!... But don't you think, maybe, we were victims of some hallucination?

Alas! I'm afraid not!... I found a great circle of burnt grass on the terrace this morning!...

Heavens, Blake! Don't tell me you also think that...

Yes, I know. It seems preposterous! So, better to drop the subject for the moment... Instead, let's go back to the story of how you made your discovery so we can know where we stand... We've had little chance to do so since last night...

Well! As the journalists are implying (and even though I deliberately left some of these details out of my letter), the place is, indeed, located near Povoação. It's a deep chasm that the locals call "O foro da diabo."* Intrigued by the extravagant stories about it, I decided to explore it. With the help of my guide Pépé, I descended into the chasm, and I must confess that I wasn't disappointed: The sights were worthy of the legend! Galleries, huge rooms, torrents... it was all there! Anyway, the map you're holding will tell you more than any description... I was eventually stopped by that lake. As I lacked the appropriate equipment, I was about to turn back when I suddenly caught a glimpse of something under the surface... something that looked like a peculiar concretion. With a good deal of effort, I managed to pull it out of the wall in which it was embedded, and to my immense surprise, I discovered that it wasn't a gypsum crystal as I'd originally thought but a material entirely foreign to the surrounding formations...

ENTRANCE PLAN
ROCK SLIDE
SECTION OF THE FORO DA DIABO CHASM
SLANTED ROOM
ROOM OF THE "CALDEIRAS"
ROOM OF THE GREEN LAKE
SHAFT
CRAWL
LAKE
160
-1800
-2000
-1600
-3000
?

*THE DEVIL'S ABYSS

After coming back here, I examined my find and discovered that it was no mineral I could identify—and that it had some peculiar properties. Not only was it clearly luminescent in the dark, but, what's much more important, it was also indubitably radioactive!... As I pondered this conundrum, I must confess I couldn't help but think of orichalcum, the Atlanteans' mysterious metal that was as precious as gold!!...

Here we are!!...

But you seem to have neglected the fact that, according to Plato, this extraordinary orichalcum was used to craft jewellery and household items, and even to build defensive walls. I have a hard time imagining such things being radioactive!...

Of course I raised the same objections myself, and I concluded that only a more complete exploration of the cave would let us verify this crazy theory! That's why I asked you to join me here to help me solve this mystery, old friend.

All right! Count on me, old boy! All the more because we're not the only ones interested in that metal!...

Good show, Francis! I knew you'd agree! I'll call my guide Pépé immediately. We should be ready in four or five days!

FIVE DAYS LATER, AT DAWN, BLAKE AND MORTIMER ARE DRIVING FAST ON THE ROAD TO POVOÇÃO. PREPARATIONS FOR THE EXPEDITION HAVE BEEN MADE SWIFTLY, AND IN ORDER TO THROW JOURNALISTS AND POTENTIAL SPIES OFF THE SCENT, PÉPÉ HAS BEEN INSTRUCTED TO ASSEMBLE THE EQUIPMENT AND PORTERS IN A SECRET PLACE.

Phew! I do believe we've finally managed to lose that pack of jackals. Reporters!...

Haven't they tried to get our guide to speak?

Of course they have! They even attempted to bribe him. But that good man told them that we wouldn't be leaving 'til next week... We can trust him!...

AND YET, AT THAT VERY MOMENT, THE "GOOD MAN" IS HAVING AN INTERESTING CONVERSATION WITH THREE FELLOWS DRESSED UP AS LOCALS. ONE OF THEM IS NONE OTHER THAN THE INFAMOUS OLRIK...

Is not very honest, what I'm doing. Hiring you instead of my porters!

I'm telling you, these gentlemen and I are journalists! Come, now. This should be enough to silence your scruples... And don't worry about the rest!...

FIVE MINUTES LATER...

Hello, laddies!

Careful, now! Call me Luis!...

WITH THESE WORDS, AND AFTER HIDING THE CAR, THE SMALL CARAVAN IS UNDERWAY, LEAVING BEHIND THE BEAUTIFUL FURNAS VALLEY.

AFTER A CAREFUL REVIEW OF HIS TROOPS, MORTIMER TURNS TOWARDS THE GUIDE:

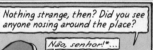

Nothing strange, then? Did you see anyone nosing around the place?

Não, senhor!*...

And you will vouch for your assistants, of course?...

My assistants?... Er!... Naturalmente, senhor...

*NO, SIR!

BUT NEITHER BLAKE NOR MORTIMER SUSPECTS THAT ONE OF THE TEAM'S MEN IS IN RADIO CONTACT WITH TWO INDIVIDUALS HIDDEN A COUPLE OF MILES AWAY, INSIDE A SHEPHERD'S HUT...

You're leaving?... OK... Be careful... Understood!...

THE SUN HAS NOW FULLY RISEN. AFTER AN EXHAUSTING WALK, THE SMALL PARTY HAS FINALLY REACHED THE ENTRANCE TO THE CHASM AND IMMEDIATELY SETS UP CAMP THERE... FULLY DECKED OUT, OUR TWO FRIENDS ARE GETTING READY FOR THE TRIP DOWN. BUT OLRIK, WHO'S GOING WITH THEM, SWIFTLY SLIPS OVER TO ONE OF HIS ACCOMPLICES...

You're ready, Francis. Go ahead!

Keep an eye on Pépé... And if he should think about changing his mind...

Understood!...

MEANWHILE, THE MAN WITH THE WALKIE-TALKIE IS CALLING...

He's managed to get chosen for the trip down instead of Pépé... No, they don't suspect a thing... Very well!... I'll let you know...

Understood, then? If the weather shows signs of changing, call us right away!

De acordo, senhor*...

MORTIMER HAVING JOINED BLAKE, OLRIK, WITH A LAST INTENT LOOK AT HIS MEN, FOLLOWS THEM DOWN INSIDE THE GAPING HOLE...

... WHILE INSIDE THE SHEPHERD'S HUT, IT'S TIME FOR REJOICING...

Well, Kurt, I think this one's a done deal!...

*VERY WELL, SIR.

AFTER A 150-FOOT DESCENT, OLRIK HEARS THE PROFESSOR CALL HIM.

Ho, Luis! Are you OK?

Sim, muito bem, senhor!*

*YES, VERY WELL, SIR.

SOON JOINED BY THE SO-CALLED LUIS, THE TWO MEN BEGIN MAKING THEIR WAY DOWN THE ROCK SLIDE ON WHICH THEY'VE LANDED...

Onwards...

GOING FIRST, MORTIMER WALKS RESOLUTELY WHILE UNCOILING A TELEPHONE WIRE...

How on Earth can you be making your way forward so boldly?

Thanks to these ribbons of Scotchlite I carefully placed to mark my path during my last visit... When the light from my torch sweeps over them, they become luminescent.

HAVING REACHED THE BOTTOM OF THE FIRST ROOM, MORTIMER STOPS BEFORE A NARROW OPENING IN THE GROUND.

This is the shaft! Be especially careful as you go down. The rock is rotten. It crumbles and breaks off at the merest touch...

FIFTEEN MINUTES LATER, AFTER THEY'VE GOT DOWN WITHOUT A HITCH, MORTIMER WATCHES "LUIS" ARRIVE...

One moment! Our abseiling rope is caught on...

BUT, STOPPING IN MID-SENTENCE, HE SUDDENLY GRABS HIM AND SLAMS HIM AGAINST THE WALL.

Move!!!

AT THAT MOMENT, A LARGE ROCK NARROWLY MISSES THE PROFESSOR'S BACK AND SHATTERS ON THE BOTTOM OF THE SHAFT, SENDING PIECES FLYING IN ALL DIRECTIONS.

BROOM

Well! Luis, lad, that was a close one!...

Er!... I... I... Deus te paghe, senhor!!*...

By Jove! This blasted place is full of dangers!

No doubt... But it also has its compensations. Look at this!...

IN THE LIGHT OF MORTIMER'S MAGNESIUM TORCH, AN IMMENSE ROOM UNVEILS ITSELF... A FANTASTIC CHAOS OF TITANIC ROCKS, WITH JETS OF SULPHUROUS VAPOURS SPOUTING HERE AND THERE BETWEEN THEM!...

*GOD BLESS YOU, SIR!

Heavens! I feel like I'm looking at Dante's Inferno!... What are these vapours?

This is what they call "As Caldeiras do Inferno*" here. When the weather is wet or stormy, they become extremely dangerous, for the vapours then fill the entire cave, making the air unbreathable. Then, woe betide the careless explorer who finds himself in this place!...

*HELL'S CAULDRONS

Why didn't we bring masks, if this is so?

Because they would be completely useless to us. The vapours are opaque and would make it impossible to get our bearings. Suffocating or getting hopelessly lost would be our only choices!

AT THAT PRECISE MOMENT, AT THE ENTRANCE OF THE CHASM, PEPE IS CASTING A WORRIED EYE ON THE SKY...

Desconfio dissa nuvem!!!*

6

*I DON'T LIKE THE LOOKS OF THAT CLOUD!

MEANWHILE, 2,000 FEET BELOW THE SURFACE, THE THREE MEN HAVE RESUMED THEIR PROGRESS. CLIMBING OVER GIGANTIC ROCK PILES, GOING FROM MARK TO MARK, THEY MAKE THEIR WAY TOWARDS THE BACK OF THE ROOM. FINALLY, AFTER SLIPPING BETWEEN TWO GREAT SLABS, THEY STOP BEFORE THE MASSIVE, FEATURELESS WALL...

See, Francis; we must reach that crawl there...

Hmm! It looks rather uninviting!...

HELPED BY HIS COMPANION, MORTIMER QUICKLY CLIMBS TO THE ENTRANCE...

Hnh! I'm there!...

... THEN BLAKE AND THE SO-CALLED LUIS JOIN HIM WITHOUT A HITCH, USING A ROPE HE'S THROWN THEM.

FINALLY, THE THREE OF THEM START CRAWLING DOWN THE NARROW TUNNEL...

A SHORT WHILE LATER, THE SMALL TEAM IS GATHERED ON A VAST LEDGE HALFWAY UP THE SHEER WALL OF A LARGE BOWL. ON THE BOTTOM, THE TRANSPARENT WATERS OF A LAKE GLIMMER GENTLY...

Is this it?

Yes... Go ahead—you'll find the equipment I left here on my first trip... As for me, I'm going to establish communication with Pépé...

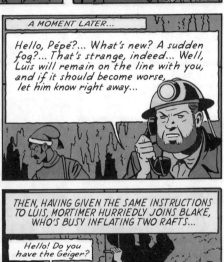

A MOMENT LATER...

Hello, Pépé?... What's new? A sudden fog?... That's strange, indeed... Well, Luis will remain on the line with you, and if it should become worse, let him know right away...

PROGRESS IS SLOW AND EXHAUSTING. THEIR FACES TENSE WITH THE EFFORT, THEIR CHESTS AND SHOULDERS CONSTRICTED, THEIR HELMETS SCRAPING AGAINST THE ROCK, THE THREE MEN STRUGGLE CONSIDERABLY... AT LAST, AFTER 60 FEET OF ARDUOUS CRAWLING, MORTIMER PULLS HIMSELF AWAY FROM THE NERVE-RACKING EMBRACE OF THE ROCK WITH ONE LAST EFFORT. IN A BREATHLESS BUT TRIUMPHANT VOICE, HE UTTERS THE TRADITIONAL WORDS...

... I'm through!!!...

THEN, HAVING GIVEN THE SAME INSTRUCTIONS TO LUIS, MORTIMER HURRIEDLY JOINS BLAKE, WHO'S BUSY INFLATING TWO RAFTS...

Hello! Do you have the Geiger?

Don't worry, everything's here!

It's unsettling. Looking up at these sheer walls, I can't help but be acutely and frighteningly reminded of how much we depend on the people we left on the surface...

Ha, ha! Are you getting claustrophobic?... Come on, let's get to work!

HAVING PUSHED THEIR RAFTS INTO THE WATER, THE CAPTAIN AND THE PROFESSOR SLOWLY BEGIN TO FOLLOW THE NARROW SHORE...

There! This is about the spot where I found the shard!

Well, let's search the lake methodically. If that doesn't yield any results, we'll go have a look inside the tunnel...

SLOWLY, THE TINY BOATS BEGIN CRISS-CROSSING THE CALM WATERS. SOON, THREE-QUARTERS OF THE LAKE HAVE BEEN SEARCHED...

It'd be quite unbelievable if there was only one specimen here of...

Shhh! Listen!

INDEED, THE GEIGER COUNTER HAS JUST BEGUN TO EMIT ITS CHARACTERISTIC SOUNDS.

BOP BOP BOP

ALERTED, THE TWO MEN ATTEMPT TO LOCATE THE ORIGIN OF THE RADIATION...

We must be very close now...

Yes... A little more to the left...

There! See that pale glow!...

Hurray! This is what we were looking for!...

BUT, FROM THE ENTRANCE TO THE CHASM, PÉPÉ SUDDENLY GIVES A FRANTIC CALL.

Hello!... Ah! Porfim!... I have been calling for 15 minutes... You must come back right now!... The sky, it is getting darker all the time... There is a tempestade coming!... Hello!?... Hello!...

HOWEVER, UNAWARE OF THE THREAT BREWING ABOVE HIS HEAD, MORTIMER HAS STEPPED OUT OF THE BOAT WITHOUT HESITATION.

Do you think you can work it loose?...

Yes. Fortunately, the water isn't deep here.

BAFFLED BY THE SO-CALLED JOURNALIST'S APPARENT APATHY, PÉPÉ TRIES AGAIN...

Senhor!... Senhor Luis!... Quick! Call the Professor! We already hear thunder... Hello!?!...

BUT OLRIK, GREEDILY FIXATED ON OUR FRIENDS' EVERY MOVE, ISN'T REALLY LISTENING TO THE DELUGE OF WORDS FROM THE GUIDE.

What?... Oh, yeah, a storm brewing?... All right, I got it! No need to shout like that!... OK!...

AFTER A GREAT DEAL OF WORK, MORTIMER MAKES ONE LAST EFFORT, AND...

Well! What do you think of this?!

Extraordinary!!

PÉPÉ, STUNNED BUT TENACIOUS, PERSISTS.

Ma, senhor, por amor di Deus*, understand me: You must come back this second! The storm, it is about to start!... The vapores!... The vapores!!!

* BUT, SIR, FOR THE LOVE OF GOD

OLRIK, THOUGH, IS FASCINATED BY THE MYSTERIOUS ROCK. IRRITATED, HE TURNS OFF THE TELEPHONE.

Enough blabbering!... Besides, they're coming back anyway...

Hello, Luis! Any news?

No, senhor... er... Oh, except that Pépé, he says the storm is here, and...

What? The storm's here and you just lay there without warning us? Come on, we can't afford to dawdle! But first, you're going to hoist this rock up there.

A MOMENT LATER, THE ROCK, SAFELY TUCKED INSIDE A SACK...

All right, heave!

...SLOWLY RISES TOWARDS THE LEDGE.

We'd better make sure we hang onto it this time!

Oh, I'm not worried about that. What does worry me are those damned "caldeiras."

I've got it... and I've got them!!!

All right! And now, secure the ladder and drop the rope back to us!

Immediatamente, senhor!

AND SUDDENLY...

There you go, gentlemen... ladder and rope!!!

8

LIKE A DEMON, OLRIK PEELS OFF HIS DISGUISE AND STANDS UP ON THE LEDGE...

Ha! Ha! Ha! Do you recognise me, my good friends?!... Colonel Olrik, at your service!!!

BLAKE AND MORTIMER, AGHAST AT THE SUDDEN REAPPEARANCE OF THEIR INDOMITABLE ENEMY, ARE DUMBSTRUCK...

Olrik!?!...

Olrik!?!...

This time, boys, you're done for! No supplies, and a nice storm coming for you!... You're going to be trapped like rats in their hole! Ha! Ha! Ha!

As for your pebble, it's in good hands! We'll make good use of it!

BUT WHILE THE INSOLENT CHARACTER GOES ON THUS, BLAKE INSTINCTIVELY BENDS DOWN TO PICK UP A ROCK, AND...

... WITH A STRENGTH AND SKILL BOLSTERED BY ANGER, HE SUDDENLY THROWS IT AT OLRIK.

Take this, you knave!!

STRUCK IN THE FOREHEAD, THE SCOUNDREL STAGGERS...

Ow!!!

... AND, BLINDED BY THE PAIN, DROPS THE PRECIOUS BAG THAT BOUNCES DOWN THE CLIFF.

By the devil! Your victory will be short-lived, my masters! I will come back to feast on the sight of you in your dungeon once you're finally out of the picture!... Adieu!

AS QUICKLY AS HE CAN, OLRIK RETRACES HIS STEPS THROUGH THE CRAWL. BUT AS HE MAKES IT BACK INTO THE ROOM WITH THE GIANT ROCK SLIDES, HE DISCOVERS WITH DREAD THAT, WITH THE STORM, THE WHOLE CAVE IS FILLING WITH SUFFOCATING VAPOURS...

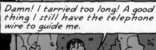

Damn! I tarried too long! A good thing I still have the telephone wire to guide me.

HALF-CHOKING, STUMBLING AT EVERY STEP, HE BEGINS FOLLOWING THE WIRE. BUT THE PATH IS TREACHEROUS, AND...

AS HE REACHES THE TOP OF A ROCK PILE, HE SLIPS ON A RIDGE AND FALLS BACK!

WHEN HE FINALLY MANAGES TO STOP HIS FALL, HE DISCOVERS WITH TERROR THAT HIS CLENCHED FIST NOW GRIPS ONLY THE SEVERED END OF THE WIRE...

Broken!!! I'm done for!...

FACED WITH THAT TERRIBLE REALISATION, OLRIK HAS LEAPT TO HIS FEET. HE TRIES TO FIND HIS BEARINGS, BUT HIS LAMP HAS GOT LOST IN HIS FALL, AND THE CHOKING SULPHUROUS EMANATIONS THAT KEEP BUILDING UP ARE MAKING HIS EFFORTS MOOT. COUGHING, TEARS POURING FROM HIS EYES, HE WANDERS IN A HAZE OF RAGE AND TERROR...

I can't breathe!!.... Ah! I'll never get out of this hell!!...

BUT, SUDDENLY, SOUNDING AS IF IT COMES FROM BENEATH THE EARTH, A CALL RESOUNDS ALMOST AT HIS FEET...

?

HEY

HO

IT IS A WORRIED PÉPÉ WHO HAS COME DOWN TO THE ENTRANCE OF THE CALDEIRAS ROOM DESPITE THE DANGER AND IS CALLING OUT TO HIS COMPANIONS FROM THERE.

Hey, ho!

FILLED WITH RENEWED HOPE, ORLIK ANSWERS.

HEY, HO!

BUT, TO HIS ASTONISHMENT, THE RESPONSE HE RECEIVES SEEMS TO BE COMING FROM ABOVE HIM THIS TIME!

HEY, HO

?

DUMBFOUNDED, HE CALLS OUT ANEW. THIS TIME, PÉPÉ'S VOICE SEEMS TO BE COMING FROM HIS LEFT...

?!

HEY

HO

KNOWING THAT THIS IS HIS LAST CHANCE, HE GIVES A MIGHTY BELLOW.

HEY, HO!!!

ALAS, PÉPÉ'S ANSWERS COME TO HIM FROM ALL DIRECTIONS NOW...

Curses!!!

HEY HO HEY HO HEY HO

SEIZED BY COMPLETE PANIC, OLRIK UNDERSTANDS THAT HE IS THE VICTIM OF ONE OF THOSE CURIOUS ACOUSTIC PHENOMENA PECULIAR TO CAVES. MAD WITH FEAR, HE RUSHES FORWARD BLINDLY...

HEY

HO

Help! Help me!!!

BUT HE HAS TAKEN ONLY A FEW STEPS WHEN HE FEELS THE GROUND DROP AWAY FROM BENEATH HIM. WITH ONE LAST CRY, HE IS SWALLOWED BY A GAPING CHASM!...

AH!!

WHILE THE TREACHEROUS OLRIK, HOISTED WITH HIS OWN PETARD, VANISHES INTO THE DEPTHS, BLAKE AND MORTIMER ARE STILL ON THE SHORE OF THE GREEN LAKE AND, AFTER SEVERAL FAILED ATTEMPTS, HAVE GIVEN UP ON CLIMBING THE HIGH WALLS THAT SURROUND THEM ON ALL SIDES...

It's impossible! Unless we try to carve some stairs into the rock...

That'd take us days! And we have no provisions and our lights won't last much longer... And it would be pointless to expect any sort of help from the outside!

The only choice we have, then, is to either wait for death here or try our luck down that narrow tunnel over there!...

TURNING AROUND SUDDENLY, THOUGH, BLAKE CUTS HIM OFF...

Too late! The decision has been made for us!!!

Good Lord! The caldeiras!

Back! Back!...

INDEED, BELCHING FORTH FROM THE CRAWL AS WELL AS FROM A HUNDRED CRACKS, THE YELLOW CURLS OF THE SULPHUROUS VAPOURS ARE BEGINNING TO POUR INTO THE BOWL... HASTILY GRABBING SOME OF THEIR EQUIPMENT, BLAKE AND MORTIMER HURRY BACK TO THEIR INFLATABLE RAFTS.

This way, Francis!

WITH A FEW STROKES OF THEIR PADDLES, THE TWO FRIENDS HAVE MOVED AWAY FROM IMMEDIATE DANGER AND ARE HEADING TOWARDS THE TUNNEL ENTRANCE...

Quick! In a moment we won't be able to see a thing!...

Just in time! The lake's almost completely disappeared!

I don't understand! These phenomena don't usually occur on such a scale!

CARRIED FORWARD BY A SLOW CURRENT, THE RAFTS GLIDE SILENTLY UNDER THE LOW, DARK CEILING OF THE UNDER-GROUND STREAM. WHEN, AFTER A QUARTER OF A MILE...

Well! Listen to the Geiger: There must be some orichalcum around here!

Indeed, I can see a pale gleam ahead... and two more a tad further!...

AS THEY DRIFT ONWARDS, THE MINERAL OUTCROPS BECOME MORE AND MORE NUMEROUS, UNTIL THE ENTIRE RIVER HAS BECOME LUMINESCENT...

By Jove! We must have found the mother lode!

BUT MORTIMER, WHO'D BEEN LOOKING AT THE CEILING FOR SOME TIME, COMMENTS...

Look, it's getting lower and lower! Not a good sign!

INDEED, THE TWO MEN SOON DISCOVER THAT THE CEILING, HAVING GOT LOWER STILL, HAS REACHED THE SURFACE AND DISAPPEARS BELOW IT...

I knew it... A siphon!...

Goodness! What shall we do? We don't have any diving equipment!...

Well!... We don't have much choice. I'm going to go have a look... Let's hope it's negotiable!...

HAVING QUICKLY UNDRESSED, MORTIMER HAS GONE INTO THE WATER, A ROPE TIED AROUND HIS WAIST...

We're agreed, then. One tug: "Give me some slack." Two: "I'm through." Three: "I'm coming back." Several: "I'm in trouble."

All right.

AND THE PROFESSOR DIVES INTO THE ICY WATER.

BLAKE IS FOCUSED ON THE ROPE THAT SWIFTLY PLAYS OUT BETWEEN HIS FINGERS.

One... One... One... Again!... one, two! Ah, he must be through!...

What's keeping him, then?... Ah, finally! One... two... three... he's coming back! Oh, but what's this?... Four... five... Good Lord!!

PUTTING ALL HIS STRENGTH INTO IT, BLAKE IMMEDIATELY HAULS ON THE ROPE TO BRING HIS COMPANION BACK. BUT IT RESISTS HIS MIGHTIEST EFFORTS...

Heavens! What happened to him?!...

11

The rope must have caught on something!... There isn't a moment to lose!...

AND, WITHOUT HESITATION, BLAKE DIVES, KNIFE IN HAND. BUT, TO HIS SURPRISE, THE WATER IN THE SIPHON TURNS OUT TO BE CLOUDY WITH MUD...

WITH VISIBILITY LIMITED TO ONLY A FEW INCHES AHEAD, HE FOLLOWS THE ROPE THAT LINKS HIM TO HIS COMPANION, SWIMMING AS FAST AS HE CAN...

SUDDENLY HE SEES HIM, STRUGGLING CONVULSIVELY TO FREE HIMSELF FROM THE ROPE THAT HAS GOT SNAGGED AND TRAPPED HIM...

UNDERSTANDING THE SITUATION IN AN INSTANT, BLAKE PUTS HIS KNIFE TO THE LINE, AND...

... PUSHING THE HALF-CONSCIOUS PROFESSOR AHEAD OF HIM, HE BRINGS HIM BACK TO SAFETY...

Hold on, old chap!

Glug!

A FEW MINUTES LATER...

... Everything went well until I turned back. By then, the mud I'd dislodged from the walls and bottom on my way forward had rendered the water too murky to see. Unable to get my bearings, I began going around in circles. And that was when the rope got snagged somewhere... Goodness gracious, that was close!...

I'll say!... But what about the siphon?...

Passable!... Some 25 yards, and then the river goes on and widens...

Perfect! Let's go, then. I'm freezing!

FIFTEEN MINUTES LATER... THE PROFESSOR AND THE CAPTAIN HAVE SUCCESSFULLY NEGOTIATED THE SIPHON. THEN, HAVING DRIED THEIR EQUIPMENT AS BEST THEY CAN, THEY'RE GETTING READY TO CONTINUE THEIR FORAY INTO THE UNKNOWN...

So? Shall we go on?...

As if we had a choice!

THEY HAVE FOLLOWED THE TWISTING COURSE OF THE RIVER ALONG ITS LAZY CURRENT FOR TWO HOURS WHEN, SUDDENLY, THE WATER BEGINS TO BOIL!...

What does this mean?...

... EVEN AS ITS COLOUR GRADUALLY TURNS CRIMSON...

Look! It's turning red!

Some strange volcanic phenomenon, no doubt. It...

Listen!...

A LOW RUMBLING RISES FROM THE CENTRE OF THE EARTH, CAUSING THE CAVE'S WALLS TO QUIVER!

BRRRRRROOMMMMMM!!!

Blimey! An earthquake!

Well, that's all we need...

BUT MORTIMER CANNOT FINISH HIS SENTENCE...

Damn! What's this?!?...

THE TWO RAFTS ARE SUDDENLY CAUGHT IN A NEW, MUCH STRONGER CURRENT...

?

... WHICH, DESPITE ALL THEIR EFFORTS, CARRIES THEM INCREASINGLY QUICKLY...

I can't seem to slow down this blasted raft!...

We're caught in rapids!...

... TOWARDS A TUNNEL, THE ENTRANCE OF WHICH IS DEFENDED BY A VERITABLE PORTCULLIS OF STALACTITES AND STALAGMITES...

Heavens! We're going to get smashed against those rocks!

MORTIMER BARELY HAS TIME TO FLATTEN HIMSELF AT THE BOTTOM OF THE RAFT BUT MANAGES TO SCRAPE THROUGH!...

!

BLAKE, WHO IS HEADING STRAIGHT FOR A STALAGMITE, AVOIDS CRASHING INTO IT WITH A WELL-TIMED PUSH OF HIS PADDLE—BUT IT IS SHATTERED IN THE PROCESS!

!

CRACK

WITHOUT ANY MEANS TO SLOW IT DOWN, THE CAPTAIN'S RAFT RUSHES HEADLONG INTO THE TUNNEL, PASSING MORTIMER.

Blake! What's going on?

My paddle broke!!!

AS THE FLOW OF WATER BECOMES EVER FASTER AND MORE TUMULTUOUS, A DISTANT THUNDER BEGINS TO SOUND, GROWING MORE MENACING BY THE MINUTE...

MORTIMER, WHO IS VAINLY TRYING TO CATCH UP TO BLAKE, YELLS:

Blake, look out! A waterfall!!!!

DESPITE THE CAPTAIN'S DESPERATE EFFORTS, HIS OUT-OF-CONTROL SKIFF CONTINUES INEXORABLY ON ITS COURSE...

THE SOUND OF THE WATERFALL IS NOW DEAFENING! CAUGHT IN AN EDDY, MORTIMER IS THROWN ONTO THE BANK AND STUMBLES TO SAFETY!...

... WHILE BLAKE IS DRIVEN STRAIGHT ONTO A GROUP OF EMERGED ROCKS ON THE EDGE OF THE ABYSS!

Goodness! He's doomed!

THE IMPACT IS BRUTAL! BLAKE IS THROWN INTO THE WATER...

... WHILE THE RAFT TUMBLES INTO THE HOWLING DEPTHS...

MIRACULOUSLY, BLAKE MANAGES TO GRAB A ROCK AND HANG ON!...

Mortimer! Help!...

15

FROM THE NARROW BANK, MORTIMER SHOUTS:

I'm coming, Blake! Grab this!...

AND WITH UNERRING ACCURACY, HE THROWS A ROPE THAT BLAKE CATCHES.

HNH!

HAVING TIED THE ROPE TO THE ROCK, THE CAPTAIN HANGS ON FOR DEAR LIFE AS HE CROSSES THE RIVER...

Almost there, old fellow!

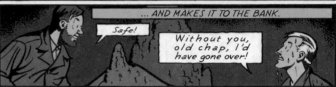

... AND MAKES IT TO THE BANK.

Safe!

Without you, old chap, I'd have gone over!

Unfortunately, we're still not out of the woods. All my equipment is gone!

As for me, I managed to salvage a pick, a torch, and this rope...

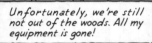

Let's hope it'll be long enough to allow us to make it down the waterfall. I think that's our best option...

I think so too. Besides, I think I can see some sort of beach over there!

AND OUR FRIENDS BEGIN RAPPELLING DOWN THE SHEER WALL.

THE DESCENT IS UNEVENTFUL.

Blast! We're going to have to swim to the bank!

Hey! This water's scalding hot! We're going to get boiled alive like lobsters!

All the more reason to hurry!

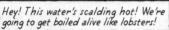

HAVING QUICKLY REACHED A SHALLOW AREA, THE TWO MEN WALK ASHORE ONTO A LARGE PEBBLE BEACH SURROUNDED BY A VERTICAL ROCK WALL. AS FOR THE RIVER, IT DISAPPEARS INTO A MASS OF ITS OWN SEDIMENT, ALONG WITH THE WATER'S LUMINESCENT PROPERTIES!

Blimey! What a sinister place!...

Feels like the end of the world!

Hmm. This time, I'm afraid we really are stuck!

Let's see! There's got to be some sort of opening somewhere...

BUT THE PROFESSOR CASTS THE LIGHT OF HIS TORCH ONTO THE SHEER, EMPTY WALL IN VAIN...

Nothing... Not even a mouse hole...

It's a big cave. Let's look somewhere else...

Yes, but this torch can't have more than another hour of life in it. If we haven't found a way out by then, we'll end up starving to death in the dark.

What a lovely th...

BUT AT THAT MOMENT, A LOW AND MENACING RUMBLE SHAKES THE ENTIRE ROOM. ROCKS TUMBLE AND SHATTER WITH THUNDEROUS CRACKS, WHILE THE GROUND SPLITS INTO GIANT FISSURES!!!!

BRRRRRROOMMM!

FOR MANY LONG MINUTES, ROCK SLIDES FOLLOW COLLAPSES. THE TERRIFYING TREMORS TURN THE HUGE CAVE INTO A MASS OF FALLEN BOULDERS.

AT LAST, EVERYTHING SEEMS TO HAVE SETTLED DOWN. BLAKE, WHO HAS TAKEN REFUGE BEHIND A GIGANTIC STALACTITE, STANDS UP AND CALLS OUT FOR HIS COMPANION.

Mortimer! Mortimer!...

TO HIS TREMENDOUS RELIEF, A DISTANT VOICE ANSWERS FROM DOWN INSIDE A FISSURE...

Where are you?

Blake! Down here!!!

THE CAPTAIN HURRIES TO THE CRACK.

Hello, old chap! Are you hurt?

No, nothing broken!... But come down here!...

On my way! I just need to let down this rope!

BLAKE LOWERS HIMSELF DOWN INTO THE FISSURE...

Thank God you're all right!... But what's this glow? I thought it was your torch!...

My torch is in pieces. Tell me what you think of this place!...

Well, I'll be!... This gallery seems to be manmade...

That's what I thought, too. But let's go on—the light is coming from further away.

AS THEY PROGRESS THROUGH THE DEBRIS, THE LIGHT BECOMES BRIGHTER AND BRIGHTER, UNTIL THEY REACH THE OTHER OPENING...

By Jove!

Incredible!

BEFORE THEM IS A VAST, STRAIGHT TUNNEL, ITS LUMINESCENT WALLS DUG INTO THE MYSTERIOUS MINERAL STRETCHING INTO INFINITY...

A mine! An orichalcum mine!!!

Yes, there's no doubt now!...

CAUGHT UP IN THE THRILL OF THE DISCOVERY, THE PROFESSOR FEVERISHLY STROKES THE BRIGHT OUTCROPPINGS...

What a marvel this is, Francis!

BUT SUDDENLY, HE STAGGERS...

Damned!... The radiation!

BLAKE RUSHES TO HIM AND DRAGS HIM INTO A DARK TUNNEL...

This way! We have to get out of this blasted maze as soon as we can...

JUST THEN, A STRONG GUST OF AIR HITS THEM IN THE FACE...

A draft!?... But, that means there's a way out somewhere!

Chin up! We're saved! This gallery leads outside!...

Too late! This radiation is not of the benign kind!...

KEEPING HIS WORRIES IN CHECK, BLAKE WALKS UP THE CORRIDOR, SUPPORTING HIS COMPANION...

Just a little longer! I can see a faint light!...

CARRIED BY A LAST BURST OF ENERGY AND HOPE, THE TWO MEN RAPIDLY COVER THE LAST FEW YARDS, AND...

Confound it! This isn't the surface!...

INDEED, THEY HAVE JUST ARRIVED ONTO A SORT OF SMALL OVERHANG, 300 FEET ABOVE A GIGANTIC CANYON BATHED IN A STRANGE RED GLOW...

There must have been a sort of natural bridge here once...

SUDDENLY, BLAKE SWAYS ON LEGS TURNED TO RUBBER. OVERWHELMED BY A STRANGE DIZZINESS, HE LETS GO OF THE PROFESSOR'S ARM, LETTING HIM COLLAPSE.

What on earth?!?...

The radiation!!... It's affecting me too, now!...

AS HE ATTEMPTS TO FIND HIS BALANCE, HE STEPS CLOSER TO THE EDGE OF THE CLIFF. UNDER HIS WEIGHT, A LARGE BLOCK OF STONE SNAPS OFF THE OVERHANG AND PLUMMETS INTO THE CANYON WITH A DEAFENING RUMBLE...

... NO SOONER HAS THE STONE SMASHED INTO THE RIVER AT THE BOTTOM OF THE CHASM THAN A STRANGE SOUND RISES IN RETURN...

... AND ALL OF A SUDDEN, WITH A CACOPHONY OF DISCORDANT CRIES, A FLOCK OF GREAT, BLACK, BIRD-LIKE THINGS APPEARS, CARRIED BY THEIR POWERFUL WINGS!...

HORRIFIED, BLAKE IS QUICKLY FACED BY A DEMONIC-LOOKING CREATURE!

Pterodactyls!!!

SHAKING OFF THE DEADLY TORPOR THAT SMOTHERS HIM, HE LEAPS TO MORTIMER'S SIDE, TRYING TO RECOVER THE PICK TUCKED INTO THE PROFESSOR'S BELT...

BUT, SNAPPING THEIR TEETH-FILLED JAWS, THE MONSTERS SWARM OVER HIM... IN THE WILD MELEE THAT FOLLOWS, BLAKE'S SHOULDER IS LACERATED, AND A CLAW LEAVES A DEEP GASH IN HIS LEG...

AS HE COLLAPSES UNDER THE RAIN OF BLOWS, IT SEEMS TO HIM THAT THE AIR IS SUDDENLY FILLED WITH BLINDING RAYS OF LIGHT, BUT...

... AT THAT MOMENT, HE RECEIVES A MASSIVE BLOW TO THE FOREHEAD, AND EVERYTHING TURNS DARK.

WHEN BLAKE AND MORTIMER, SLOWLY TEARING THROUGH THE VEIL OF VAGUE AND FRIGHTENING DREAMS THAT HAVE BEEN GRIPPING THEM, FINALLY COME TO THEIR SENSES, THEY FIND THEMSELVES IN AN EXTRAORDINARY PLACE...

BUZZING SOFTLY, AN ASSORTMENT OF STRANGELY SHAPED PROJECTORS IS DIRECTING A FLOOD OF MYSTERIOUS AND RESTORATIVE RAYS AT THEM...

Blake!... Are you there?

Yes, I'm here!

ASTOUNDED, THEY SIT UP AND GAZE ABOUT...

By Jove! Where on earth are we?

And what's the meaning of these strange clothes?

THE TWO MEN FRANTICALLY TRY TO PIECE THEIR MEMORIES BACK TOGETHER...

Wait!... I think I remember... I believe we were wandering through endless corridors...

BUT THEY HAVE NO TIME TO REFLECT FURTHER, FOR, JUST AS THE PROJECTORS SWIFTLY PULL AWAY, A STRANGE DOOR OPENS SILENTLY BEFORE THEM...

... AND REVEALS A MAN WHOSE DEMEANOUR IS FORMAL AND SOLEMN... EVEN SOMEWHAT UNNERVING...

SEEING HIM, BLAKE AND MORTIMER HAVE STEPPED FORWARD...

I say! Sir, will you tell us where we are and who you are?...

Yes!... And know that we find very little humour in this tomfoolery!...

BUT NEITHER REMARK SEEMS TO DISTURB THE NEWCOMER IN ANY WAY, AND HE SIMPLY RESPONDS COLDLY:

Follow me...

Goodness! It feels like being in a science-fiction film!... What should we do?

Well, we don't have much choice. Let's go!...

AND, THEIR LEGS STILL A TAD WEAK, THEY FOLLOW THEIR GUIDE AND WALK OUT THE DOOR, WHERE TWO DOCTORS ARE STANDING GUARD.

They don't seem very sure of themselves!... I wonder what will become of them?...

I don't know. But one thing I'm sure of is that if the phulacontarkos* had been with the patrol that rescued them from the pterodactyls, he'd have ordered that they be left to their fate!...

*CAPTAIN OF THE GUARD

AFTER HAVING TREKKED THROUGH A MASSIVE LABYRINTH OF STAIRS AND CORRIDORS, THE THREE MEN RIDE A MONUMENTAL ESCALATOR INTO A VAST AND MAGNIFICENTLY ADORNED HALL...

... AT THE FAR END OF WHICH A MAN IN RICH CLOTHING STANDS BEFORE AN ENORMOUS GATE.

Hail, Magon!

WITH HIS HEAVY ROD, HE STRIKES THE BRONZE DOOR THREE TIMES, MAKING IT RESOUND...

BOOMM

19

SLIDING NOISELESSLY, THE HEAVY DOOR OPENS...

... REVEALING A ROOM WHERE A MAN SITS ENTHRONED IN A GOLD CHAIR, HIS DEMEANOUR NOBLE AND IMPOSING, SURROUNDED BY RICHLY-DRESSED DIGNITARIES.

THE PHULACONTARKOS WALKS ON, FOLLOWED BY OUR TWO FRIENDS. HAVING REACHED THE FOOT OF THE DAIS AND SALUTED, HE SAYS:

O Basileus! Here are the prisoners!

THE ONE WHO HAS JUST BEEN HAILED EMPEROR, ALBEIT BY THE ANCIENT FORM OF THE TITLE, SPEAKS UP IN A DEEP VOICE.

You, Professor Mortimer, and you, Captain Blake, who have been rescued from the monsters of the abyss by one of our patrols and healed from mortal radiation by our doctors; Magon, our phulacontarkos, holds you for dangerous spies...

AT THAT MOMENT, MAGON EXCLAIMS WITH PASSION:

That's the absolute truth, o Basileus! These villains snuck into our territory with the sole intention of bringing about our downfall!

MORTIMER'S TEMPER FLARES AT THESE WORDS...

You ruddy liar! How dare you?!...

Philip!

What?! You insult me!!!

Peace, Magon!

BUT A YOUNG MAN OF NOBLE BEARING INTERVENES...

I personally watched the endeavours of these men on the surface. Scientific curiosity alone drove them to mount this expedition, and I will vouch for the purity of their intentions!

Is that so?! This show of trust seems rather bizarre and foolhardy to me... Watch out, Prince, that you do not make yourself the accomplice of their evil plans!...

Enough! My decision is made! These men seem sincere to me. However, it is out of the question that they ever leave the underground abode where their boldness has brought them. The professor and the captain will remain our guests for the rest of their lives!...

Surely you cannot really think of doing this!

We're British citizens, and...

My decision is final!...

TURNING TO THE YOUNG MAN, THE BASILEUS CONTINUES...

My nephew, I place them in your care... You'll answer for them before the Council. Treat them as friends...

Thanks be to you, o Basileus!

I am the Aerostrategos of the Air Fleet. Do not worry. I will look after you!

UNDERSTANDING THAT THEY MUST RESIGN THEMSELVES FOR THE MOMENT, BLAKE AND MORTIMER FOLLOW THE YOUNG MAN OUT OF THE ROOM. BUT MORTIMER, NO LONGER ABLE TO CONTAIN HIS IMMENSE CURIOSITY, CRIES OUT:

But, Prince, will you tell us at last where we are?...

Gladly...

You're in Atlantis!!!...

LIGHTNING STRIKING THE GROUND AT THE TWO MEN'S FEET WOULD NOT HAVE SHOCKED THEM AS MUCH AS THE PRINCE'S REVELATION...

A... Atlantis?!!... You must be joking?...

Atlantis!... Surely, you don't mean...

Come!...

AND PRINCE ICARUS, WITHOUT GIVING THEM TIME TO SAY ANY MORE, QUICKLY LEADS THEM AWAY. STUNNED BEYOND WORDS, BLAKE AND MORTIMER FOLLOW HIM THROUGH A SUCCESSION OF CORRIDORS UNTIL THEY REACH A LARGE ROOM FULL OF BUSY PEOPLE, THE WALLS COVERED IN MAPS.

THE YOUNG MAN HEADS STRAIGHT FOR A WIDE BAY WINDOW AND SAYS...

Behold Poseidopolis, our capital!... May it dispel your doubts!...

THERE, BEFORE THE WONDER-FILLED EYES OF THE VISITORS, AN ENORMOUS, FANTASTIC CITY UNFOLDS AS FAR AS THE EYE CAN SEE. FROM THE DISTANT CEILING HIGH ABOVE EMANATES A MYSTERIOUS GLOW THAT BATHES THE WHOLE CAVE IN A LIGHT SIMILAR TO THAT OF THE SUN. ALL THE WHILE, MEN ON STRANGE VEHICLES MOVE THROUGH SPACE, GOING UP AND DOWN AND EVEN FLOATING IN PLACE LIKE MOSQUITOES...

AFTER A LONG, SPEECHLESS MOMENT, BLAKE FINDS HIS VOICE...

Come, now!... All those historians who admit that Atlantis wasn't just a mythical empire agree that it disappeared beneath the waves without a trace...

My friends, what have men of science not agreed upon since the beginning of time?

Look at this map, if you will. This is the island of Atlantis 12,000 years ago! The yellow represents the land swallowed by the cataclysm; the orange is for the parts still emerged nowadays...

NORTH AMERICA

40°

ATLANTIS

Azores

EUROPE

30°

Madeira

Canaries

20°

Sargasso Sea

AFRICA

Cape Verde

... Yes, it did, indeed, sink beneath the ocean after a horrifying disaster caused by the arrival in our solar system of a giant comet. However, by a strange twist of fate, the disaster miraculously spared a number of our ancestors. They survived, and had to struggle to deserve it...

THEY WERE A GROUP OF SAGES AND ASTRONOMERS AMONG THE MOST DISTINGUISHED, GATHERED AT THE OBSERVATORY OF MOUNT POSEIDON—CURRENTLY PICO ISLAND—SO AS TO STUDY THE STRANGE PHENOMENA THAT WERE BEGINNING TO WORRY THE PEOPLE...

... FOR AT THE SAME TIME AS A STRANGE LIGHT HAD APPEARED IN THE SKY, THE GOVERNORS OF THE VARIOUS PROVINCES OF THE EMPIRE HAD STARTED REPORTING DISTURBING EVENTS: EARTHQUAKES, VOLCANIC ERUPTIONS, ABNORMAL TIDES, DEVASTATING STORMS, ETC...

... FINALLY, ONE NIGHT, THE COMET APPEARED ON THE HORIZON, GROWING SWIFTLY WITH EVERY PASSING HOUR...

BLAKE AND MORTIMER, ABSOLUTELY FASCINATED BY THE STORY, HANG ON TO THE NARRATOR'S EVERY WORD... (19)

THREE DAYS AFTER IT APPEARED, THE COMET HAD REACHED GIGANTIC PROPORTIONS. ITS BLINDINGLY BRIGHT TAIL SEEMED TO COVER HALF THE SKY. AND ON EARTH, THERE WERE MORE AND MORE DISASTERS!...

... EARTHQUAKE FOLLOWED EARTHQUAKE WITHOUT PAUSE. EVERY VOLCANO WAS SPEWING FIRE AT ONCE. TIDAL WAVES RAVAGED THE SHORELINES. ISLANDS EMERGED FROM THE OCEAN AND OTHERS VANISHED. THE PANIC THAT HAD GRIPPED THE PEOPLE NOW BORDERED ON MADNESS!... AND YET, THE TERRIBLE EFFECTS THAT THIS VISITOR FROM SPACE HAD WROUGHT UPON EARTH WERE NOTHING COMPARED TO THE UPHEAVALS IT HAD CAUSED WITHIN OUR PLANETARY SYSTEM...

FOR, BACK THEN, THE MOON WAS AN INDEPENDENT PLANET, AND A SMALLER SATELLITE ORBITED OUR WORLD. NOT ONLY DID THE GIANT COMET FORCE THE MOON INTO EARTH'S ATTRACTION, BUT IT ALSO CAUSED THE SMALLER SATELLITE'S ORBIT TO LOWER!...

... UNTIL WHAT WAS BOUND TO HAPPEN, HAPPENED. SUDDENLY, ON THE FOURTH DAY, AROUND THE TWELFTH HOUR, THE SMALL SATELLITE FELL INTO THE OCEAN!!

... THE SHOCK MADE THE EARTH WOBBLE. ENTIRE ISLANDS AND WHOLE CHUNKS OF CONTINENTS DISAPPEARED. A MONSTROUS WAVE WENT AROUND THE GLOBE SEVERAL TIMES, SWEEPING EVERYTHING IN ITS PATH!... FROM THE HEIGHT OF THEIR OBSERVATORY, THE HANDFUL OF TERRIFIED SCIENTISTS AND THEIR FAMILIES COULD ONLY WATCH IN HORROR AS POSEIDOPOLIS, THE SUPERB CAPITAL OF THE EMPIRE, WAS WIPED OUT, ALONG WITH THE PRESTIGIOUS ATLANTEAN CIVILISATION!!...

IT WAS ONLY LATER THAT THE SURVIVORS, AS THEY GAZED AT THE VAST, MUDDY SEA THAT LAY WHERE THE CAPITAL HAD BEEN AND THE WAVES THAT WERE NOW BATTERING THE CRUMBLING WALLS OF THEIR REFUGE, FULLY UNDERSTOOD THE FULL SCALE AND MEANING OF THE CATASTROPHE...

... THESE PROUD MEN, WHO HAD RULED OVER THE WORLD, COULD NOT ACCEPT THEIR FALL. RATHER THAN REQUEST ASYLUM FROM THEIR FORMER VASSALS, THEY DECIDED TO HEAD DOWN INTO THE BOWELS OF THE EARTH, THERE TO FOUND A NEW EMPIRE, ONE BASED IN KNOWLEDGE AND WISDOM.

AND SO, AFTER MILLENNIA SPENT PURSUING PROGRESS AND ADVANCEMENT, THE ATLANTEANS HAVE REACHED THEIR CURRENT LEVEL OF GREATNESS. AND ALL THE WHILE, THEY HAVE OBSERVED, FROM DEEP INSIDE THEIR UNDERGROUND HAVEN, AS MANKIND WENT CEASELESSLY FROM WAR TO REVOLUTION.

I must confess that since you've succeeded, like us, in releasing the energy of the atom, our people are rather worried. For we know what you are ready to use it for!!!...

AT THESE WORDS, MORTIMER, WHOSE FERTILE IMAGINATION HAD BEEN RECREATING IN HIS MIND ALL THE PRODIGIOUS IMAGES OF ICARUS'S STORY, STUMBLES BACK INTO THE PRESENT AND REALITY.

Indeed! And on that subject, will you explain the mystery of radioactive orichalcum?... For I assume that it is a metal, is it not?

Exactly! In ancient times, we used it to make our weapons, our jewellery, and many other things. It suddenly acquired these strange properties as it came into contact with our small satellite when it fell from the sky.

... Now, it's become for us an inexhaustible source of energy. Energy that powers, among other things, the crafts we use to explore interplanetary space and, more importantly, to keep an eye on the activities of men. Those crafts are what you call...

... FLYING SAUCERS!?!?...

BUT AT THAT INSTANT, A PIERCING BUZZER SOUNDS...

One moment!...

THE AEROSTRATEGOS QUICKLY WALKS TO A LARGE COMMAND CONSOLE, SURMOUNTED BY A HUGE SPHERE CEASELESSLY ROTATING AND TILTING. INSIDE THE SPHERE IS A SORT OF FOG...

Who's calling, Arios?

Two ships from the 3rd Stolos* are requesting reentry, Strategos.

*SQUADRON

SUDDENLY, THE SPHERE CEASES ALL MOTION, THE FOG DISSIPATES, AND TWO "FLYING SAUCERS" APPEAR INSIDE THE DEEP BLUE SCREEN, AS VOICES COME OUT OF THE SPEAKERS...

Hello, this is Alpha 4. Awaiting orders. Over!

This is Delta 7. Awaiting orders. Over!

THE COMMANDER OF THE AEROKASTRON* ANSWERS IMMEDIATELY:

Hello! This is the Aerokastron. Reduce speed to 2,000 mph; descend to 120,000 feet. Over!

*CONTROL TOWER

BLAKE AND MORTIMER, WHO HAVE COME CLOSER AS WELL, FOLLOW WITH ASTONISHMENT THE EVOLUTIONS OF THE SHIPS, THEIR THREE-DIMENSIONAL IMAGES SEEMING TO COME OUT OF THE SPHERE!

Descending to 120,000 feet. I...

ALL OF A SUDDEN, AS IF HE WAS TRYING TO EVADE A PURSUER, ALPHA 4 BREAKS TO THE RIGHT, WHILE AN ANGUISHED VOICE CALLS OUT...

Look out! We're...

BUT THE VOICE IS CUT OFF BY A BLINDING FLASH OF LIGHT FOLLOWED BY A THUNDERING EXPLOSION, AND THE SHIP IS BLOWN TO SMITHEREENS BEFORE THE HORRIFIED EYES OF THE SPECTATORS...

! !

Hello! Hello! Delta!... What happened?!!!...

I... I don't know... I was nearly destroyed by the blast!...

It was Kafit flying Delta 7, wasn't it? Have him report to me as soon as he's back...

Yes, Strategos!

THE PREOCCUPIED PRINCE LEAVES THE AEROKASTRON, FOLLOWED BY BLAKE AND MORTIMER...

An... An accident?

Probably... but a strange one, indeed. It's the third we've had in less than two weeks!

AN HOUR LATER. WHILE PRINCE ICARUS IS SHUT UP IN HIS OFFICE WITH THE PILOT OF DELTA 7, THE TWO FRIENDS ARE WAITING IN THE GALLERY THAT OVERLOOKS THE HALL.

It's taking a while...

Yes. It's obvious that something isn't right. Ah! Look...

KAFIT, THE PILOT, HAS JUST COME OUT OF THE OFFICE AND IS CASTING FURTIVE GLANCES ABOUT HIM AS HE WALKS.

WHEN THE TALL SILHOUETTE OF MAGON APPEARS FROM BEHIND A COLUMN AND MOTIONS HIM OVER...

... THE MAN IMMEDIATELY, BUT FURTIVELY, HEADS TOWARDS THE FORMIDABLE OFFICIAL...

JUST THEN, PRINCE ICARUS LEAVES HIS OFFICE AND MAKES HIS WAY DOWN THE HALL.

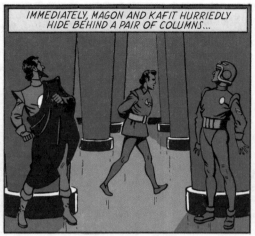

IMMEDIATELY, MAGON AND KAFIT HURRIEDLY HIDE BEHIND A PAIR OF COLUMNS...

THEIR CURIOSITY RISING, BLAKE AND MORTIMER LEAN DOWN, THE BETTER TO WATCH THEIR ACTIONS. BUT THIS TIME, THE PHULACONTARKOS HAS SEEN THEM...

Careful! We're being watched!...

Those two surfacers are definitely too nosy... We're going to have to take terminal measures...

OUR TWO FRIENDS HAVE NO CHANCE TO SEE MORE, FOR AT THAT MOMENT ONE OF THE PRINCE'S SERVANTS ARRIVES.

My master invites you to share his meal. He's had some clothing prepared for you as well. I'll show you to your quarters...

Lead the way.

AN HOUR LATER, COMFORTABLY SETTLED IN A ROOM DECO-RATED IN ELEGANT AND DELICATE FRESCOES, SURROUNDED BY WARM LIGHT, THE CAPTAIN, THE PROFESSOR AND THE PRINCE ARE FINISHING THEIR DINNER... FRUITS, REFRESHING DRINKS, AND STRANGE DELICACIES FILL THE TABLE...

That was quite delicious!

Yes, exquisite!...

I'm glad you think so. True, we have a strictly vegetarian diet, but it's of high quality, thanks to our artificial cultivation techniques. They're based on chemical fertili-sation and accelerated vitamin-infusing processes...

Fascinating!... And yet, there's one thing that seems even more surprising to me: How is it that you speak our language?...

There is no great mystery there. Every member of the High Council is fluent in 10 or 12 of the most important surface languages. A secret process, which is reserved for the ruling caste only, actually implants that knowledge in them. It begins during childhood and requires no effort...

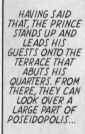

HAVING SAID THAT, THE PRINCE STANDS UP AND LEADS HIS GUESTS ONTO THE TERRACE THAT ABUTS HIS QUARTERS. FROM THERE, THEY CAN LOOK OVER A LARGE PART OF POSEIDOPOLIS...

See, beyond the city limits, Atlantis spans an immense system of massive caves linked by galleries, canals and lakes, themselves lined with outposts, ports and power plants. It was on the outskirts of this vast territory that you were rescued. What you see over there on the left is the nuclear plant, and that enormous mass all the way in the back is the old dam. It's no longer in use, but in the past it was used to bring in the seawater we needed to pro-duce our energy...

As for us, we're inside the palace that holds all the command and security centres of Atlantis, the basileus's residence, and the astronautical department.

Speaking of which... Among the phulacontarkos's duties, are there any related to astronautics?...

None... But why do you...

HE HASN'T EVEN FINISHED HIS SENTENCE WHEN A LONG SPRAY OF BLINDING FIRE STRIKES THE PARAPET!!!

24

MORTIMER JUMPS ASIDE, SLIGHTLY SINGED BY SPARKS FROM THE MYSTERIOUS FIRE THAT HAS JUST DISINTEGRATED PART OF THE PARAPET. BUT ICARUS HAS LOOKED UP, AND NOW CRIES OUT...

There!... They must have shot from that porthole!!!

WASTING NO TIME, THE PRINCE DASHES TO A LIFT, FOLLOWED BY THE TWO MEN...

Quickly!

TEN SECONDS LATER, THEY COME OUT INTO AN OCTAGONAL GALLERY, LIT BY THE LONG, HORIZONTAL OPENING THEY'D SEEN FROM BELOW, AND IN FRONT OF WHICH A PLUME OF SMOKE STRETCHES SLOWLY...

See! Our attacker did act from here!...

Aside from the lift, this place only has one exit: the passage. Therefore, he must have left in that direction! Come on!!!

QUICKLY, THEY RUN DOWN A DARK, SPIRALLING RAMP...

Oh, wait until I get my hands on that scoundrel!

JUST AS THEY ARRIVE AT THE ENTRANCE TO A HALLWAY, THEY CATCH A GLIMPSE OF A DOOR CLOSING SWIFTLY AT THE OTHER END...

There! We've got him!...

CLAP

IN MOMENTS, THEY ARE AT THE DOOR...

It's open!

Careful!...

... BUT HAVING GONE THROUGH, THEY FIND THEMSELVES INSIDE A COMPLETELY DARK ROOM.

Watch yourselves! He must be hiding somewhere...

Hold on; I'll try to...

BUT, SUDDENLY, THE LIGHTS COME ON, FLOODING THE ROOM, AND THE PURSUERS FREEZE IN PUZZLEMENT. MAGON, FLANKED BY TWO ARMED PHULOS*, IS STANDING ON TOP OF A STAIRCASE.

What's this? Prince Icarus and the noble foreigners!

Magon!?!

? ?

*GUARDS

I beg of you, gentlemen: Next time, make your arrival known!... I almost mistook you for ill-intentioned visitors and was about to treat you as such! I would have been very sorry if I had!

Forgive us, Magon, if we entered your sector by accident... But the fact is that we were chasing a man who had just attempted to murder us!

My word! An assault inside this palace? This is unthinkable!... I will immediately launch an inquiry. I assure you, Prince, and you gentlemen from the surface, that I will apply all my vigilant zeal to this case!

LETTING THE MATTER DROP, ICARUS LEAVES WITH BLAKE AND MORTIMER. BUT HE LOOKS TROUBLED.

THEN HE STOPS IN HIS TRACKS, AS IF STRUCK BY A SUDDEN THOUGHT.

Say, why did you ask that question about the phulacontarkos's duties just before the... the incident?

Goodness... That was probably nothing... We saw the pilot you'd just debriefed furtively join Magon—who was himself hiding while waiting.

THE PRINCE REMAINS PENSIVE FOR A WHILE, THEN SAYS:

My friends, I think it'd be wise for you not to leave your quarters for a while...

MEANWHILE, THE PHULACONTARKOS IS GIVING KAFIT, WHO'S JUST COME OUT OF HIS HIDING PLACE, A FIERCE TALKING-TO...

You clumsy fool! You almost ruined everything!!!

But, Contarkos... If I missed them, it's because you instructed me to make sure the prince wouldn't get hurt!!!

23

A FEW HOURS LATER... A MILITARY SPHEROS, TRANSPORTING A SQUAD BACK FROM PATROL DUTY, SETTLES ONTO ONE OF THE PALACE'S LANDING PADS...

... WHERE THE RELIEF SQUAD AWAITS. THE TWO COMMANDING OFFICERS GREET EACH OTHER GAILY...

Hail, Theodos. Welcome to Poseidopolis. Anything to report over there?...

Nothing! Except that I'm quite happy to be done with it for a few days!

WITH THIS, THE OFFICER BIDS HIS FELLOW FAREWELL AND LEADS HIS SMALL PARTY TOWARDS THE PHULOS BARRACKS...

... WHERE, SHORTLY AFTERWARDS, HE REPORTS TO MAGON.

Hail, Contarkos!

Hail, Theodos. What news?...

THE OFFICER PULLS OUT A STRANGELY DECORATED ARROW FROM UNDER HIS CLOAK AND HANDS IT TO HIS COMMANDER.

This...

Oh?

MAGON GRABS IT AND SWIFTLY UNSCREWS IT IN THE MIDDLE...

Let's see!...

A SMALL SKIN SCROLL THAT WAS HIDDEN INSIDE FALLS OUT.

THE CONTARKOS IMMEDIATELY UNROLLS IT, REVEALING A STRANGE-LOOKING MESSAGE...

... WHICH HE BEGINS TO DECIPHER...

Good old Tlalac.

By Zeus! Can it be true!?... Surely he was sent by the gods of the underworld!!!

Good news, my Lord?

Good?... It's beyond anything I could have hoped for!... The time is near, Theodos. But first... There's something we have to do... and quickly!... Tell Kafit to come right away.

MEANWHILE, BLAKE AND MORTIMER HAVE FOLLOWED ICARUS'S INSTRUCTIONS AND RETIRED TO THEIR QUARTERS. MORTIMER, MARVELLING AT THE SURPRISING PROPERTIES OF THE WATER THAT FEEDS INTO THEIR POOL, HAS CONVINCED HIS FRIEND TO TRY IT AS WELL.

You have to admit, these people know how to make a fellow feel welcome... Aside from the occasional assassination attempt, of course!

As for that, did you know that Icarus had two guards placed at our door? That way...

BUT, SUDDENLY, MORTIMER'S EARS PRICK UP...

Hey! Listen... That must be him coming back...

It can't be... The noise didn't come from the door...

Well? Was I right? Isn't this water marvellously invigorating?

Extraordinary! And so pure, despite its opacity! It must come from some volcanic spring...

Panel 1:
INDEED, TWO MEN, EACH WEARING A HELMET AND A STRANGE APPARATUS ON HIS BACK, HAVE JUST SNUCK INTO OUR FRIENDS' FLAT THROUGH A WINDOW.

Panel 2:
ONE OF THEM IMMEDIATELY GOES TO LOCK THE FRONT DOOR.

Better plan for everything!

Yes, good thinking.

Panel 3:
I hear nothing. Could they be sleeping?

Sleeping or not, we have to act fast and not give them time to raise any alarm. Let's go!

Panel 4:
HAVING FLIPPED SWITCHES ON THEIR CHEST-MOUNTED CONTROL PANELS, THE TWO SINISTER INDIVIDUALS BEGAN FLOATING ABOVE THE GROUND. THEN, ACCOMPANIED BY A LOW DRONING SOUND, THEY BEGIN MOVING ABOUT THE ROOM LIKE FISH IN THE SEA...

Panel 5:
WITH SMOOTH MOTIONS THAT MAKE THEM LOOK LIKE NIGHTMARISH MONSTERS, THEY SYSTEMATICALLY EXPLORE THE QUARTERS, ROOM BY ROOM.

Nothing!

No one here!

Panel 6:
Only the bathroom's left...

All right, watch it, then!...

Panel 7:
THE DOOR SLIDES OPEN QUIETLY, BUT...

Empty!?!

That's impossible! They haven't left their quarters. I'm sure of it!

Panel 8:
SLOWLY, THE FLYING MEN PASS OVER THE POOL, CHECKING EVERY CORNER...

Panel 9:
BUT, HAVING FOUND NOTHING, THE TWO CONFOUNDED INTRUDERS STOP TO PONDER THE SITUATION...

What are we going to tell him? He's going to be furious!

Yes, especially since Tlalac demands that they be executed before...

Panel 10:
SUDDENLY, ONE OF THE MEN EXCLAIMS:

Look! Their clothes!...

What? But then, they...

Panel 11:
BUT AT THAT MOMENT, THE FRONT DOOR IS SHAKEN ENERGETICALLY...

Blake!... Mortimer!... It's me!... Open the door!!... Ho!...

Panel 12:
Curses! Here they come!

Too late... Let's go!

Shoot off the lock!!

A LONG JET OF FIRE IS ALREADY SLICING THROUGH THE THICK DOOR...

Panel 13:
... AND THE TWO MEN BARELY HAVE TIME TO JUMP OUT THE WINDOW!!

A SECOND LATER, THE PRINCE AND HIS MEN BURST INTO THE BATHROOM JUST AS BLAKE AND MORTIMER, HALF DROWNED, SPRING UP FROM UNDER THE OPAQUE WATER WHERE THEY'D BEEN HIDING FROM THEIR ENEMIES.

Alive! Zeus be praised!

Phew! Just in time...

One more second and my lungs would have burst!

WHILE THE GUARDS SEARCH FOR CLUES, THE TWO FRIENDS QUICKLY INFORM ICARUS OF WHAT HAS TRANSPIRED...

Unfortunately, we didn't get a chance to see our visitors...

We only heard a droning sound and whispered voices!

Droning sound? Oh! That means they were using "planos"*...

What about the whispering? Could you make out any words?

It was so indistinct...

Wait... I risked lifting my head out of the water briefly and heard something like... Halak, or Balak...

*PLANOS: INDIVIDUAL FLYING EQUIPMENT

THE LAST WORDS MAKE ICARUS START...

Are you certain of what you say? Think... It's very important! Could it have been Tlalac instead?

Yes... I think so... Something like that, anyway.

THE PRINCE APPEARS THROWN INTO UTTER CONFUSION BY THAT ANSWER...

Tlalac... Tlalac!? Might it be?... Oh, I have to know for sure! It's too terrible a thought!...

FOR A WHILE, THE YOUNG MAN APPEARS LOST IN THOUGHT... THEN, TAKING A SNAP DECISION, HE SAYS:

Gentlemen, I'm going to have to leave for a few days. I must investigate all of this in greater detail...

Let us come with you. The air in this palace isn't really healthy for us!

And we could be of more use to you wherever you go...

I don't know if I have the right to expose you to more dangers. On the other hand, who knows what they might do to you in my absence?... Very well, you're coming with me!

AN HOUR LATER...

Well, dear fellow? Do I make a good phulos?

Superb! You look like a true Atlantean!

THE PRINCE ENTERS...

My friends, I must warn you that our mission is of extreme importance, which means it could be equally dangerous. Are you still ready to follow me?

Yes!

Yes!

THE THREE MEN LEAVE THE ASTRONAUTICAL DEPARTMENT IN SECRET THROUGH A SERIES OF HIDDEN PASSAGES...

... AND SOON REACH A LANDING STAGE, WHERE TWO GUARDS OF PROVEN VALOUR WAIT FOR THEM NEAR A SPHEROS.

WITH THE SMALL GROUP ABOARD, THE CRAFT SLOWLY SLIDES OUT OF THE TUNNEL...

... AND SUDDENLY, THE INCREDIBLE MACHINE, LIKE A BUBBLE OF SHINY GLASS, RISES IN THE AIR.

WHAT THE FIVE COMPANIONS DON'T KNOW IS THAT MAGON HAS WATCHED THEM LEAVE THROUGH A POWERFUL TELESCOPE HIDDEN BEHIND A PORTHOLE.

It's them, no doubt about it!

MEANWHILE, MAKING GOOD TIME, THE SPHEROS SOON REACHES THE EDGES OF THE GIGANTIC CAPITAL CITY...

... AND FLIES INTO A MASSIVE TUNNEL.

We're almost at Migos, the end of the aerial lines. There, we'll switch to a different mode of transportation.

SOON AFTER, IN THE AIR TERMINAL'S CONTROL TOWER...

Are my instructions clear?

Absolutely, Contarkos. And here they come now...

HAVING ABANDONED THEIR FLYING VEHICLE, THE PRINCE AND HIS COMPANIONS CLIMB ABOARD A WAITING ROBOT-CONTROLLED MONORAIL.

LEAVING IMMEDIATELY, THE MONORAIL ACCELERATES QUICKLY AND IS SOON SPEEDING FORWARD...

HOURS GO BY. IT PASSES THROUGH A BARREN AREA DOTTED WITH STRANGE RUINS...

There are the remains of monuments built long ago by the barbarians our ancestors fought off.

The barbarians? What barbarians?

The descendants of the wild people who lived on the borders of Atlantis at the time of its end, and whom we colonised...

After the disaster, several of their princes joined us in our voluntary exile. But after a few centuries, they became aggressive, and their actions brought the new Atlantis to the brink of destruction. They had to be fought for a long time. They were finally pushed back far from here and have been held at bay ever since. Unfortunately...

AT THAT MOMENT, THE CHIEF CONTROLLER AT MIGOS STATION, WHO'S BEEN FOLLOWING THE PROGRESS OF THE MONORAIL SINCE ITS DEPARTURE, SUDDENLY PULLS A LEVER...

THE VEHICLE, WHICH WAS ABOUT TO NEGOTIATE A BEND, IMMEDIATELY JUMPS ITS RAIL! THROWN INTO THE AIR...

... IT SMACKS INTO A ROCK FACE AND, WITH A HORRENDOUS DIN, COMES CRASHING DOWN AT THE BOTTOM OF A STREAM.

Well, that's that!!!

SHORTLY AFTERWARDS, MAGON, LOCKED INSIDE HIS OFFICE, LISTENS TO HIS HENCHMAN'S REPORT, TRANSMITTED FROM THE MIGOS CONTROL TOWER.

... as the monorail I was remotely controlling reached the bend, I... followed your orders! The car fell into the stream, but by some miracle, the prince, the two surfacers, and one of the guards survived unharmed. At this moment...

Curses!

... A RESCUE MONORAIL IS LEAVING THE CRASH SITE WITH THE FOUR SURVIVORS ON BOARD.

Well! They can thank their lucky stars!

TWO HOURS LATER, AT OMEGARA—LAST ATLANTEAN OUTPOST...

Hail, Prince! I'm glad to see you safe after this unfortunate accident.

Thank you, Phokis. Alas, I lost one of my best men...

But, tell me, is our tank ready? We must continue on our way as soon as possible...

Of course! It's being brought out now.

ON THE GROUNDS OUT FRONT, SEVERAL MEN ARE BUSYING THEMSELVES AROUND A POWERFUL-LOOKING TANK.

Did you have the necessary equipment loaded aboard?

It's all there, Strategos. You have supplies for at least 10 days.

JUST BEFORE TAKING OFF, ICARUS QUICKLY WHISPERS TO THE GARRISON COMMANDER:

We'll stay in contact with you, but do not let anyone enter this sector!

Understood!

AND THE VEHICLE DRIVES AWAY, DISAPPEARING QUICKLY...

It's a hunting trip, then, is it?

So I hear... I wonder what kind of game they'll bring back!

FOR MANY LONG HOURS, THE TANK PROGRESSES ALONG THE LUMINESCENT ROAD THAT SNAKES THROUGH THE BARREN SCENERY. HERE AND THERE, THE RUINS OF ANCIENT BARBARIAN CITIES ARE STILL VISIBLE.

Hello! Omegara!... We're at point Lambda 2. Nothing to report. Over!

AS THEY ADVANCE EVER FURTHER INTO THE DESERTED WASTES, THE PRINCE BEGINS SPEAKING.

My friends, I think it's my duty to enlighten you fully about the goal of this expedition... At first, I believed that some unknown enemy was after you alone. But, now everything seems to point towards a much more extensive plot—a threat against Atlantis itself!

Surely not?!

What?!

... Yes, and I'm convinced that the key to this mystery lies at the border with the barbarian kingdom, to which we are now very close. Take these weapons; they could come in handy...

Ah! I'll feel much better with this little toy at my side!

Thank you, Prince.

BACK AT THE PALACE, THE TRAITOR MAGON AND HIS HENCHMEN, HUNCHED OVER A RADAR SCREEN, HAVE KEPT THEIR EYES ON OUR FRIENDS THE WHOLE TIME...

Ha! Ha! They think they'll be safe by switching frequencies... But we've got other means! Where are they?

Nearing the Sacred Gong.

THE TANK RUMBLES ON, ITS PASSENGERS UNAWARE OF THE DANGER. SUDDENLY, MORTIMER EXCLAIMS:

Look at that!!!

LIKE SOME BIRD OF ILL OMEN, A FLYING MAN HAS JUST ZIPPED BETWEEN TWO MASSIVE, COLLAPSED WALLS...

A planos!... Here?! That's not normal! We've got to get a closer look... Forward, Aribal!

Yes, sir!

VEERING OFF THE ROAD, THE TANK RUMBLES THROUGH A FIELD OF ROCKS, HEADING TOWARDS THE SPOT WHERE THE SPY IS HIDING.

Drat! They've seen me!

There! Behind that wall!

IMMEDIATELY, HUGGING THE GROUND, THE MAN FLIES OFF TOWARDS HIS NEARBY LAIR INSIDE A RUIN...

I must warn the contarkos at all costs!

FROM THERE, THANKS TO A CAREFULLY HIDDEN TRANSMITTER, HE HURRIEDLY CONTACTS MAGON...

They've sighted me and are looking for me. I can see them from here!

What!?! By Tartarus! If they capture him, all is lost! Theodos, open fire! Hurry!

Yes, Lord.

SUDDENLY, WITH A TERRIFYING WHISTLE, A BEAM OF FIRE STRIKES THE ROCK NEAR THE TANK, CAUSING A TERRIBLE EXPLOSION...

TWO MORE RAYS FOLLOW IN CLOSE SUCCESSION, BRACKETING THE TANK, WHICH IMMEDIATELY BEGINS TO ZIGZAG IN AN ATTEMPT TO ESCAPE THE DEADLY THREAT.

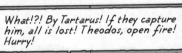

MORE STRIKES FOLLOW, THOUGH, WITH INCREASING ACCURACY—FOR, FROM HIS HIDING PLACE, THE SPY IS DIRECTING THE FIRE...

More to the right!... More!... Quick!

SUDDENLY, A SPRAY OF DESTRUCTIVE ENERGY FROM AN EXPLOSION TOO CLOSE BURSTS THROUGH THE OPENING, DISINTEGRATING THE SPOTTER IN AN INSTANT.

AT THAT MOMENT, SEEING THE RING OF FIRE TIGHTEN EVEN MORE, THE PRINCE SHOUTS:

Everyone out! Take cover... hurry!!!

OUR FRIENDS HAVE BARELY HIT THE GROUND WHEN A BLINDING BOLT OF LIGHT SLAMS INTO THE ARMOURED VEHICLE, DESTROYING IT UTTERLY ALONG WITH THE STILL-EXPOSED GUARD.

BELIEVING THAT HE'S DISPATCHED NOT ONLY THE TANK BUT ALSO THE MEN TRAVELLING INSIDE, MAGON LETS OUT A CRY OF TRIUMPH.

A hit! Good shooting, Theodos. Quick, call the planos!

BUT KAFIT'S MULTIPLE CALLS TO THE SPY ARE IN VAIN...

I can't raise him! Our man's not answering...

He must have been killed... Never mind! We don't need him anymore...

29

WITH THE STRANGE RAIN OF FIRE OVER, ICARUS AND HIS COMPANIONS BREAK THEIR COVER TO DISCUSS THEIR SITUATION...

It's just the three of us now. Fortunately, I had the presence of mind to shut off the video link before we left. Our enemy must have been following us using radar; therefore, he must be convinced he's destroyed us along with the tank. So, I propose we remain hidden and wait...

... for him to come.

That way, we'll know who we're dealing with!

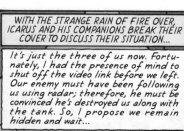

LATER, BACK AT THE PALACE, NEWS OF THE PRINCE'S DEATH HAS CAUSED QUITE A STIR...

Yes, it seems that the Omegara outpost heard distant explosions. They sent a patrol to investigate; it found the area blasted, but not a trace of the prince or his companions...

Strange!

... The prince's death is obviously going to have serious consequences for the future of the empire. He was the basileus's heir, and...

That's for certain! Speaking of which, did you know the basileus summoned Magon?

INDEED, THE ATLANTEAN RULER HAS CALLED THE PHULACONTARKOS TO HIM.

You must go there and personally lead the investigation. Icarus was on a very specific... and very secret mission!

Secret mission?... I thought he'd taken the surfacers hunting in...

That was the official line. The truth is that my nephew had discovered a very serious threat against the safety of the Empire. But, as he had only suspicions, he didn't want to say anything until he could offer the High Council solid proof of what he feared... All I know is that he intended to explore the border lands beyond the "Great Gate"! Go, then, and work swiftly! All of this must remain secret...

Count on me, o Basileus!

DESPITE HIS EFFORTS TO REMAIN IMPASSIVE, MAGON CANNOT HELP SHOWING HIS FEELINGS AS HE EXITS THE ROOM.

Look at his triumphant expression!

I'm not surprised! Icarus dead would put him a lot closer to the throne!

Not so loud! You never know...

PASSING THEODOS, MAGON WHISPERS QUICKLY.

Alert our friends. You know the place; at the third hour...

Yes, master!

AT THE AGREED HOUR, THE CONTARKOS LEAVES THE PALACE DISCREETLY AND BOARDS A CAR...

... WHICH IMMEDIATELY TAKES OFF, DASHING QUICKLY THROUGH THE INCREDIBLE LABYRINTH OF STREETS THAT CRISS-CROSS POSEIDOPOLIS...

... IT SOON ENTERS THE TUNNEL LEADING TO THE RESIDENTIAL AREA RESERVED FOR HIGH DIGNITARIES OF THE STATE...

... AND COMES TO A STOP BEFORE THE GATE OF A RICH HOUSE STANDING IN THE MIDDLE OF A LOVELY ARTIFICIAL GARDEN.

SHORTLY AFTERWARDS, MAGON ENTERS A LARGE ROOM WHERE A DOZEN INDIVIDUALS ARE GATHERED.

Hail!

Hail to you all!

Hail!

IMMEDIATELY SURROUNDED, HE DECLARES EXULTANTLY:

I bring great news!... My lords, the time has come to act!

Speak!

Tell us!

32

Like me, you want to shake off the yoke of this hated dynasty. Like me, you refuse to follow our current tyrant in his insane project. Like me, you want to climb back to the light, take back from the surfacers the land they usurped from us, and see mighty Atlantis once again dictate its law to the world... Well, all of this is now within our grasp! Indeed, following some extraordinary circumstances I cannot explain right now, a providential ally has come to us. He has been so successful at rallying the barbarians to our cause that King Tlalac is ready to put his troops at my disposal. He only awaits my signal. What do you say?...

AN APPROVING WHISPERING FOLLOWS THIS SPEECH, BUT ONE OF THE CONSPIRATORS RAISES AN OBJECTION...

Your words fill us with joy, Magon. But aren't you afraid that the barbarians, once victory is achieved, might prove themselves... demanding? Can't we act alone?

Impossible! There are too few of us, and the basileus's prestige is still too great. A strong shock is necessary to shake up the Atlanteans' complacency.

Trust me. Let's allow them to do the... hard part. And if, afterwards, they were to prove too much of a nuisance, well, we have the means to get rid of them!

Magon is right!

Yes, yes!

Well spoken!

True!

Excellent! I'm heading out there... All must man their positions now and act quickly. The attack could come at any moment!... Oh... An armband bearing a black sun will mark our supporters. Go now!

IN THE MEANTIME, ICARUS AND HIS COMPANIONS HAVE KEPT GOING, TAKING THE LONG WAY AROUND THROUGH DARK, FORGOTTEN FOOTPATHS IN ORDER TO AVOID SEARCH PARTIES AND KEEP THEIR AS-YET-UNKNOWN ENEMY IGNORANT OF THEIR FATE... THEY HAVE JUST STOPPED ON THE BANKS OF A RIVER, ITS WATERS SWIFT AND TUMULTUOUS, WHEN ICARUS SHOUTS OUT:

A river patrol! Get down!...

A BIZARRE-LOOKING VESSEL APPEARS, CARRYING A GROUP OF PHULOS AND SWEEPING ITS SURROUNDINGS WITH POWERFUL SEARCHLIGHTS...

Where on Earth do they come from?

One of the ports along the coast...

The coast?!

Yes. Atlantis is criss-crossed by streams and rivers that pour into a vast inner sea. It's even possible to reach the capital by crossing it. Unfortunately, storms are frequent—and dangerous. But they're gone now. Come on, my friends, let's march on!

THE LONG WALK RESUMES... FINALLY, AFTER SEVERAL HOURS, THEY REACH THE MAIN ROAD, EXHAUSTED. MORTIMER IS ABOUT TO STEP ONTO IT...

At last, we'll be able to walk properly!

INDEED, AFTER A FEW MINUTES, A TALL, TIERED TOWER APPEARS, SET ON A ROCKY PEAK. HALF RUINED, IT IS CONNECTED TO THE ROAD BY A NARROW BRIDGE.

THE THREE MEN HAVE HALTED.

What is that?

The Sacred Gong!... In the past, it was the very last outpost guarding the defile through which barbarian invasions would pour into Atlantis. There's an enormous gong at the top... Thanks to some strange acoustic phenomenon, its sound could be heard all the way to Poseidopolis!

... BUT ICARUS STOPS HIM.

Stop! We'd inevitably be detected by these relays that dot the length of the road, and immediately reported! I'm afraid we must stick to the bottom of the bank. Anyway, we're almost where we need to be...

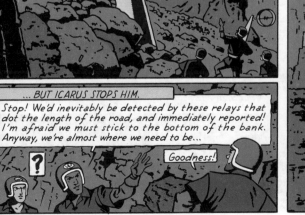

?

Goodness!

BUT BLAKE, WHO HAS BEEN CAREFULLY SCANNING THE HORIZON, INTERRUPTS...

There's movement at the entrance to the bridge!...

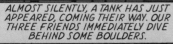

ALMOST SILENTLY, A TANK HAS JUST APPEARED, COMING THEIR WAY. OUR THREE FRIENDS IMMEDIATELY DIVE BEHIND SOME BOULDERS.

SLOWLY, THE VEHICLE ROLLS UP THE ROAD, IT'S OCCUPANTS SYSTEMATICALLY SCANNING THE SURROUNDINGS...

They're from Omegara... We can't let them see us!

THE DANGER HAVING PASSED, ICARUS, BLAKE AND MORTIMER HAVE RESUMED THEIR TRIP AND, HAVING CROSSED THE SHAKY BRIDGE THAT SPANS THE ABYSS TO LINK THE ROAD AND THE TOWER, THEY WALK THROUGH THE ARCHED ENTRANCE OF THE ANCIENT FORTRESS.

Here we'll have good cover!

Incredible!

Fantastic!

CAREFULLY, THEY MAKE THEIR WAY THROUGH THE REMAINS OF HALF-COLLAPSED ROOMS.

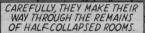

BUT ICARUS INADVERTENTLY KICKS A METALLIC OBJECT STICKING OUT OF THE GROUND...

What? A disintegrator?... What's it doing here?...

It must have fallen from a long way up to be stuck like this!

True... Ha! See... Where the ceiling's broken?

Could that be it!? That used to be the commander's quarters. Few people ever go there anymore; the stairs have collapsed! Oh, but we have to make sure...

HAVING CAREFULLY REPLACED THE SLAB, ICARUS AND HIS COMPANIONS HURRY TO THE TOP OF THE TOWER.

In case of trouble, we can go into the watch room.

This is quite the look-out post!

CAREFULLY SCALING THE RUBBLE, OUR COMPANIONS CLIMB UP TO A SMALLER ROOM WITH A STONE FLOOR. ONE OF THE SLABS IMMEDIATELY CATCHES BLAKE'S EYE...

There! See... I'll bet you...

INDEED, THE SLAB, ONCE RAISED, REVEALS A DEEP HOLE FILLED WITH VARIOUS ITEMS...

By Zeus! What's this!? Equipment! Weapons!

This looks suspiciously like a secret cache...

Maybe there are others?...

We don't have time to make sure... But if there's a cache here, it means someone intends to come back! That's an opportunity we can't miss! Let's set up camp on the terrace just above this room. From there, we'll be able to see without being seen, and we can finally identify our foes.

Good idea!

IT'S A WILD PLACE... SHEER CLIFFS, RISING ALL THE WAY TO THE CAVE'S CEILING UP IN THE SHADOWS, SURROUND THE TOWER ON ALL SIDES. ONLY A SINGLE GAP, TALL AND THIN, AND INTO WHICH THE ROAD DISAPPEARS, BREACHES THE WALL...

What's that ominous crack there?

Good heavens! What a landscape!

Arrow Pass. In the past, hordes of barbarians would pour through here, bent on destroying Atlantis... After they were finally pushed back beyond the Great Canyon once and for all, the natural bridge that spanned the chasm was destroyed and the Pass barred by a gigantic bronze gate.

I say! We've got visitors!!!

INDEED, IN THE DISTANCE A CONVOY IS APPROACHING QUICKLY ALONG THE ROAD...

IT IS THE EXPEDITION LED BY MAGON: FIVE ELECTRO-MAGNETIC REPULSION TANKS WITH NUCLEAR ENGINES, CARRYING A HUNDRED PHULOS IN FULL WAR GEAR, FLY JUST ABOVE THE GROUND AT HIGH SPEED!

Nothing to worry about on that front. I vouch for the men in the first three tanks. They're completely loyal and ready to obey blindly without asking questions.

Excellent! Theodos, make sure you send the others away on long range patrols...

Yes, Lord.

SHORTLY AFTERWARDS, THE CONVOY STOPS IN FRONT OF THE TOWER. WHILE THE MEN ARE FORMING UP, THE CONTARKOS, FOLLOWED BY THE COMMANDERS OF HIS PERSONAL GUARD, WALKS TOWARDS THE ENTRANCE...

Ha! Ha! I don't think our famed gong is going to sound the alarm all the way to Poseidopolis this time!

... AND SOON STEPS INTO THE GUARDROOM...

Here we won't be bothered.

Understood, then?... As soon as the loyalist troops are away, our men will take their prepared positions, with the goal of neutralising any troops coming from the capital. Theodos, Kafit, and 20 elite men, including 10 planos, will come with me to the other side... Should anything unexpected happen, we'll have enough firepower to stand up to anyone. A large number of the latest weapons has been stockpiled here. Every slab of...

BUT HE IS CUT OFF BY A SHOUT...

Contarkos! You must see this!!

What is it?!

THE MAN HAS JUST CAUGHT SIGHT OF THE DISINTEGRATOR OUR THREE FRIENDS UNFORTUNATELY LEFT WHERE THEY FOUND IT.

By Tartarus! What is this?!

Kafit! Take two men and go see if anyone's tampered with the cache upstairs... Have a look at the detection equipment we set up in the watch room while you're at it...

Yes, Lord!

JUST THEN, THEODOS COMES IN...

Your orders have been carried out. The unreliable elements have been sent away...

Very good. Before we get under way, though, we have one last formality to accomplish...

OPENING A SMALL CHEST, HE PULLS OUT AN ARMBAND...

Each one of you must wear this symbol of our allegiance. It will be the only distinction between friend and foe in the struggle ahead!

WHILE THE OTHERS QUICKLY DON THE BRAND OF THEIR INFAMY, THE THREE MEN SENT TO CHECK ON THE TOWER ARE COMING BACK DOWN.

Well, Kafit?

Nothing suspicious, Contarkos. One of the slabs was damaged and broke under the weight of the weapons.

Good. Let's go, then!

Oh, one last thing... Since it's always possible those barbarians might attempt some treachery, you and your planos will patrol ahead of my tank to detect any sign of an ambush.

As you order, Lord!

AND A FEW MINUTES LATER, SURROUNDED BY FLYING GUARDS, MAGON'S TANK ENTERS ARROW PASS...

After this business is concluded, we'll have to take Omegara by surprise. We can't let the garrison there raise the alarm. With the outpost in our hands, the road to the capital will be wide open!

And there's little risk that it'll resist. We'll have most of the weapons under our control, as well as the nuclear plant. Besides, our countrymen have gone soft from too much peace. They won't last long!

THE TANK TURNS A CORNER, AND THE GREAT BRONZE GATE THAT BARS THE ENTRANCE TO ATLANTIS APPEARS...

HAVING DISEMBARKED, MAGON LAYS HIS HAND ON ONE OF THE DISKS THAT ADORN THE DOOR. IMMEDIATELY, IT LIGHTS UP...

WITH THIS GESTURE, WHICH ACTIVATES A PHOTO-ELECTRIC CELL THAT IDENTIFIES THE FINGERPRINTS OF COUNCIL MEMBERS, THE GATE IS SET IN MOTION AND OPENS WIDE, REVEALING A DEEP CHASM...

Leave five phulos here. Make sure they keep their eyes peeled!

Yes, Lord!

THEN THE FLYING TANK AND ITS ESCORT CLEAR THE ABYSS AND ENTER THE FORBIDDEN ZONE.

THE CONVOY CAUTIOUSLY FOLLOWS THE ROAD LEADING TO THE ORICHALCUM WALLS. BUT, AS THEY ADVANCE DEEPER AND DEEPER, THE SURROUNDING AREA BECOMES EVER WILDER AND MORE HOSTILE, AND THE VIGILANCE OF THE FLYING INFANTRY ESCORT REDOUBLES.

We must be near the Colossal Head crossroad. I wonder...

AT THAT MOMENT, KAFIT SIGNALS OVER THE RADIO:

Tank, this is Kafit. Three men are waiting at the fork.

STANDING AT THE FOOT OF THE ENORMOUS MONOLITH THAT MARKS THE BEGINNING OF THE TRAIL LEADING TO BARBARIAN COUNTRY, THREE IMPASSIVE WARRIORS ARE WATCHING THE ATLANTEANS' APPROACH.

Peace be upon you, mighty leader! We have orders to take you to our great King Tlalac!... But he requests you only take three companions with you.

Ha! I should have known...

Don't go, Lord!... It's a trap!

Too late! We can't turn back now. You'll stay here with the tank, ready to move in at the first sign of trouble. Kafit will escort me with his two best planos.

Yes, Lord!

Very well, lead on. But do not attempt to betray us, or else...!

We do not speak twisted words, mighty leader!

WITHOUT ANOTHER WORD, THE WARRIORS START DOWN THE UNEVEN PATH, FOLLOWED BY MAGON AND HIS MEN.

AFTER A LONG TREK THROUGH THE IMPREGNABLE FIELDS OF ROCK THAT PROTECT THE BORDERS OF THE BARBARIAN KINGDOM, THE SMALL PARTY FINALLY COMES OUT INTO A KIND OF GRANITE CIRQUE, IN THE MIDDLE OF WHICH STANDS A MASSIVE TEMPLE.

What a great place for a trap!...

AT THAT MOMENT, THE HOARSE CALL OF A HORN SOUNDS OUT, SENDING ECHOES BOUNCING BETWEEN THE HIGH ROCK WALLS...

... AT THE SIGNAL, A HORDE OF ARMED WARRIORS LEAPS OUT FROM BEHIND THE ROCKS WHERE THEY'VE BEEN HIDING, SURROUNDING THE STUNNED ATLANTEANS COMPLETELY.

Curses!

ALREADY, THE VISITORS ARE READY TO SELL THEIR LIVES DEARLY, WHEN TLALAC, FLANKED BY HIS BODYGUARDS, APPEARS AT THE TEMPLE DOOR...

MAGON IMMEDIATELY ADVANCES TOWARDS THE BARBARIAN, WHO WATCHES HIS APPROACH WITH A WRY SMILE.

Hail, o king! I have come, as I promised... But why such a show of force?

I merely wanted to test the courage of my future allies... Come!

FOLLOWING THE INVITATION, MAGON AND HIS MEN ENTER THE SANCTUARY. THE HEAVY DOOR SLAMS SHUT BEHIND THEM...

Take this seat, Magon.

AND THE KING, HAVING SEATED HIMSELF, IMMEDIATELY GOES ON...

Let's not prevaricate! I've seen through your schemes, Magon!... A providential visitor has taught me everything you'd so carefully kept from me... Now I know all about the munificent wealth of the surface cities, the beauty and size of the vast empires you intend to conquer with your accursed weapons, once I and my people have allowed you to seize power. I also know that the kingdom you've promised me as a reward for my services is nothing more than an island lost in the middle of the ocean, where my people and I would be nothing more than captives dependent on your goodwill. Ha! Ha! Everything is changed, now! No more fool's bargains! To me all the lands west of the ocean, to you the ones to the east. These are my conditions!... What say you to this?...

VISIBLY SHAKEN, MAGON STRUGGLES TO ANSWER.

You... you seem strangely well informed, Tlalac... May I know the man who counselled you so well?...

Of course!

AT A GESTURE FROM THE KING, A MAN STEPS OUT OF THE SHADOWS WHERE HE IS STANDING. IT IS OLRIK! OLRIK THE MERCENARY! OLRIK, WHO WAS BELIEVED DEAD, SWALLOWED FOREVER BY THE CAULDRONS OF HELL!!!

A surfacer!?! Another one!?!

Tell your story to this lord...

TURNING TO MAGON, THE ADVENTURER DECLARES:

It was providence, really, that dropped me here at the same time it was saving my life; this way, I am now able to support and harmonise the great projects of your two people... For I am, myself, a great leader rejected by men, and I'm only waiting for an opportunity to take revenge on them! So, rest assured that you can count on me without reservation! First of all, though, you'll have to rid us of two surfacers who, I've heard...

AT THAT, MAGON, WHO'S FINALLY REGAINED HIS COMPOSURE, INTERRUPTS HIM...

If you're talking about Blake and Mortimer, be at ease. They died a few hours ago—thanks to me!

Ah! This warms my heart, because...

SUDDENLY, SHOUTS SOUND THROUGH THE DOOR, ACCOMPANIED BY FRANTIC POUNDING...

BOOM BOOM BOOM.

ENRAGED, TLALAC LEAPS TO HIS FEET AND ROARS:

Who dares!?... I want the interloper put to d...

BUT HE DOESN'T HAVE TIME TO FINISH HIS SENTENCE, FOR THE DOOR SWINGS OPEN TO LET A DISHEVELLED, HAGGARD MAN STUMBLE IN, HELD BY TWO WARRIORS... IT IS KAFIT, LIEUTENANT OF THE CONTARKOS...

Magon! We are betrayed!

AT THE SIGHT OF HIS MAN, MAGON LETS OUT A SHOUT...

Kafit!?!

BEWILDERED, THE VARIOUS ATTENDANTS HAVE NO TIME TO RECOVER, FOR AT THAT MOMENT A COMMANDING VOICE RINGS OUT:

No one move, or these three men are dead!...

THE ONE WHO HAS JUST UTTERED THESE WORDS IS NOW STANDING BEHIND THE ROYAL PARTY, HIS WEAPON POINTED AT THE CONTARKOS, WHILE HIS TWO COMPANIONS HOLD THE SHOCKED KING AND OLRIK AT BAY...

Hands up! And don't try to go for your pistol!

And now, everybody out! Except these three! Go on! Move faster!

WHEN THE ORDER IS NOT FOLLOWED QUICKLY ENOUGH, A BLAST OF FIRE STRIKES THE GROUND, SENDING THE BARBARIANS AND KAFIR INTO A HURRIED RETREAT...

They're gone! Blake, Mortimer, hurry! Close the door and lock it!

AT THESE WORDS, TLALAC, MAGON, AND OLRIK HAVE VERY DIFFERENT REACTIONS...

What? It can't be!!! That voice?...

Confound it! Them!!!... Always them!!!

May the fire of Huehueteotl strike you down!... What's the meaning of this?

Yes, Magon, you guessed right! I'm Prince Icarus! My companions and I overpowered and stripped the men you sent up the Gong Tower, where we were hiding—and from where we heard everything! I know of your treachery now, you knave! You, whom the basileus trusted! You've betrayed Atlantis to satisfy your own ambition!... But you will be punished in proportion to your crime!

Empty threats, Icarus. You'll never leave this place!

Yes, you fool! You've trapped yourself! This temple has no other exit and my men surround it! We will sacrifice you and your two accomplices to our gods!

BUT, POINTING AT A STAIRCASE LEADING TO THE CRYPT, ICARUS REPLIES:

Enough chatter. Get down there now. And move it!

UNDERSTANDING THAT RESISTING WOULD BE FUTILE, THE THREE MEN COMPLY, CONTAINING THEIR RAGE...

We'll meet again!

WORKING TOGETHER, ICARUS, BLAKE, AND MORTIMER PUT BACK THE HEAVY SLAB THAT CLOSES THE OPENING.

Now that this is done, let's see about finding a way out of here!

MEANWHILE, OUTSIDE, THE CROWD IS IN AN UPROAR. THE BARBARIANS, WHO DO NOT UNDERSTAND WHAT HAS JUST HAPPENED, SURROUND AND THREATEN THE SMALL TROOP OF ATLANTEAN INFANTRY AND TANKS THAT KAFIT HAS BROUGHT WITH HIM.

We have to do something, Theodos! We can't leave the contarkos in their clutches!

I know, Kafit. On the other hand, any action from us could be fatal to him!

IN THE TEMPLE, WHERE OUR HEROES ARE FRANTICALLY LOOKING FOR AN UNLIKELY WAY OUT, MORTIMER HAS JUST MADE A DISCOVERY.

There, see? That crack between those two blocks!

That's much too narrow for us!

Let's see...

AND ICARUS, GRABBING MORTIMER'S DISINTEGRATOR, POINTS IT TOWARDS THE OPENING, SAYING:

There are ways to remedy that. Like widening it thus... See?

HEARING THE SHOOTING, KAFIT PANICS AND SHOUTS:

Do you hear that?! They're being killed!! Break down the door!!!

IMMEDIATELY, ONE OF THE TANKS FLIES UP THE STONE STAIRS AND COMES TO A REST AGAINST THE DOOR...

THEN, APPLYING UNSTOPPABLE PRESSURE, IT PUSHES FORWARD, DISMANTLING THE DOOR AND PART OF THE WALL AND OPENING A WIDE BREACH!

KRRRAK

What?! There's no one!?!

That's impossible; they must...

AT THAT MOMENT, THE SENTRY AT THE ENTRANCE OF THE DEFILE GIVES A MIGHTY BLOW OF HIS HORN...

WOOH!

RUSHING OUTSIDE, KAFIT AND THEODOS MAKE IT JUST IN TIME TO SEE ICARUS, BLAKE, AND MORTIMER AS THEY LAUNCH THEMSELVES OFF THE ROOF...

Curses! They're getting away!!!

... AND, MAKING THE MOST OF THE CONFUSION ON THE GROUND, ZOOM TOWARDS THE ARCH...

Fire! Fire at will!!!!

THE SECOND TANK, AIMING ITS RAY EMITTER AT THE FUGITIVES, FIRES A POWERFUL SHOT...

ZZEET

BUT IT MISSES AND STRIKES THE MASSIVE ARCH INSTEAD, BRINGING IT DOWN WITH A DREADFUL NOISE!!!

BRROMM

NARROWLY AVOIDING THE DEBRIS WHISTLING THROUGH THE AIR, OUR THREE FRIENDS PUT THE SHORT RESPITE THEY'VE BEEN GIVEN TO GOOD USE AND ROCKET DOWN THE DEFILE LEADING TO THE COLOSSAL HEAD...

WHEN THE ARCH COMES CRASHING DOWN, IT TEMPORARILY BLOCKS THE PASSAGE, STOPPING THE BARBARIANS IN THEIR TRACKS EVEN AS THEY'D BEGUN CHARGING AFTER THE FUGITIVES. BUT KAFIT YELLS:

The planos after them! Now!!!

THE THREE MEN, MEANWHILE, ARE FLYING AS FAST AS THE WEAVING, NARROW DEFILE WILL ALLOW...

We'll be all right until we come out of this twisting part. Afterwards...

NO SOONER HAS HE SAID THESE WORDS THAN THE PASSAGE WIDENS INTO A LONG, STRAIGHT STRETCH. THE PRINCE AND HIS COMPANIONS PUT ON A BURST OF SPEED...

There they are!

BUT SUDDENLY, DEADLY BOLTS OF FIRE BEGIN TO TEAR THE AIR AROUND THEM.

Look out! They...

ICARUS CANNOT FINISH HIS SENTENCE...

Aah! My equipment's hit!

ITS BALANCE COMPROMISED, THE PLANOS BEGINS TO SPIN AND FALL. BUT...

... MORTIMER HAS SEEN WHAT HAS HAPPENED. SWOOPING DOWN, HE MANAGES TO GRAB ICARUS'S HARNESS...

I have you! What should I do?

Put me down as quickly as possible!

NOTICING A NARROW LEDGE, THE PROFESSOR DIVES WITH HIS COMPANION, IMMEDIATELY JOINED BY BLAKE...

... AND THE THREE OF THEM START POURING HEAVY FIRE ON THEIR PURSUERS!

A FURIOUS BATTLE BEGINS, BUT THE ATTACKERS, TOO CONFIDENT IN THEIR NUMBERS, CARELESSLY EXPOSE THEMSELVES. SOON...

... FIVE OF THEM ARE PLUMMETING DOWN, WHILE THE TWO SURVIVORS, WOUNDED, HURRIEDLY PULL OUT OF THE FIGHT...

Hurray! Good riddance to them!

Indeed. But... listen!

DOWN IN THE DEPTHS OF THE PASSAGE, A MENACING MURMUR IS GROWING...

The barbarians are coming!!!

THREE PHULOS ON DUTY AT THE ENTRANCE ARE LISTENING TO THE DISTANT SOUNDS OF THE BATTLE...

The shooting's stopped...

I'd like to know what happened!

Hey! Look, a planos!

UNWARY, THE GUARDS WATCH BLAKE CROSS THE CHASM.

Probably a messenger.

We'll soon know.

Missi baka!

Hey, friend!...

THEY ATTEMPT TO QUESTION HIM AS HE APPROACHES, BUT INSTEAD OF SLOWING DOWN, HE GIVES THE HAND SIGNAL AND THE PASSWORD, AND...

... ZIPS AWAY AT TOP SPEED, LEAVING THE THREE MEN BEHIND, TAKEN ABACK...

Er... Looks like he's in a big hurry!

I wonder if...

JUST THEN, THE POST'S RADIO CRACKLES TO LIFE. IT'S MAGON'S TANK CALLING...

Hello!... Yes, Beta 2 here... Arrest anyone that shows up? But... A planos on a special mission just came through... What?

THE UNEXPECTED ANSWER SENDS THE CONTARKOS INTO APOPLECTIC RAGE.

By Tartarus!!! Alert the tower! I want him found! I want him stopped at any costs! If he reaches Omegara, all is lost!!! But I need him alive!

Immediately, Lord!

I knew it!

REALISING THAT HE MUST ACT QUICKLY AND DECISIVELY IF HE DOESN'T WANT TO SEE HIS PLANS RUINED, MAGON DECIDES TO HEAD BACK TO POSEIDOPOLIS RIGHT AWAY.

I'm leaving without delay. Every second counts! Tlalac, you and your warriors must be ready tomorrow at the ninth hour, at the arranged place!

I will be. And woe betide the Atlanteans!

As for me, I'll take care of the other two!

AND WHILE MAGON AND TLALAC DEPART IN OPPOSITE DIRECTIONS, OLRIK SPRINGS INTO ACTION...

Search the crack... and make sure no one can reach the border without being seen. Go!

OLRIK IS RIGHT. ICARUS AND THE PROFESSOR HAVE SURVIVED THE VOLLEY OF DEADLY RAYS. INSTEAD OF DUCKING BELOW THE FIRE, THEY FLEW TO THE TOP OF THE CANYON AND THUS AVOIDED BEING CRUSHED BY THE COLLAPSING ROCKS.

You heard what they said: The attack on Atlantis is set for tomorrow at the ninth hour! If one of us hasn't managed to raise the alarm by then, the empire is lost!... I know a byroad to get back to the border, but it's such dangerous terrain to cross that I hesitate to take you through there!

Let's go, Prince! Anything's better than being trapped here like a rat in a hole!

WHILE OUR TWO FRIENDS PREPARE TO FACE NEW PERILS, BLAKE HAS REACHED THE SACRED GONG TOWER. TWO TANKS ARE PARKED NEAR THE BRIDGE, AND THE PILOT OF THE FIRST ONE BUSTLES AROUND HIS VEHICLE.

No one aside from the pilots!... The troops must be away on mission... If I could get close to... What's this!?

A VOICE SUDDENLY COMES OUT OF THE TANK'S RADIO THROUGH THE SPEAKER...

Hello! Hello! Calling all tanks! Orders are to stop a lone planos heading towards Omegara... He's a dangerous spy and must be taken alive!

By the gods!

THE MAN HURRIES BACK TO THE HATCH, BUT JUST AS HE'S ABOUT TO ENTER THE TANK, HE GLIMPSES BLAKE DIVING UPON HIM LIKE A HAWK!

!

TAKEN COMPLETELY BY SURPRISE, THE GUARD HAS NO TIME TO MAKE A MOVE...

40

A MASTERFUL UPPERCUT KNOCKS HIM OUT AND HE ROLLS DOWN ONTO THE ROAD. UNFORTUNATELY...

... THE ATTACK IS SEEN BY THE OTHER TANK'S PILOT, WHO HAS ALSO RECEIVED THE MESSAGE AND IMMEDIATELY STARTS HIS VEHICLE...

BLAKE HAS SLID INTO THE COCKPIT. AFTER A MOMENT OF DISORIENTATION, HE MANAGES TO TAKE OFF...

Ah, finally!

BUT HE DOESN'T HAVE TIME TO PICK UP SPEED: ALREADY THE OTHER TANK IS AHEAD OF HIM, BLOCKING HIS WAY...

Heavens!

... WHILE HALF A DOZEN PHULOS, ALERTED AS WELL, STORM OUT OF THE TOWER SHOUTING...

Aim for the stabilisers!

THREATENED FROM BOTH SIDES, BLAKE GOES FOR BROKE. HE PULLS HARD ON THE CONTROLS, AND THE TANK REARS AND FAIRLY LEAPS OVER ITS OPPONENT, TEARING OFF ITS SUPERSTRUCTURES, INCLUDING THE RAY EMITTER...

THROWN OFF BALANCE, THE TANK OVERTURNS, AND A GIGANTIC FLAME SHOOTS OUT, CREATING A WALL OF FIRE BETWEEN BLAKE AND THE PHULOS.

EVEN THOUGH HIS OWN TANK HAS SUSTAINED SERIOUS DAMAGE IN THE CRASH, THE CAPTAIN KEEPS GOING. GUIDED BY THE RELAYS THAT LINE THE ROAD, THE VEHICLE ROCKS AND SWERVES ITS WAY ONWARDS AT HIGH SPEED.

I won't hold out for long with so much shaking! Maybe if I try to call Omegara?...

UNFORTUNATELY, THE TRANSMITTER HAS BEEN DISABLED...

It won't work! I have to...

JUST THEN, A QUICK GLANCE BEHIND HIM REVEALS THAT HE'S BEING CHASED...

Already!?!

TURNING HIS GAZE FORWARD AGAIN, HE NOTICES OTHER TANKS HEADING TOWARDS HIM...

Too late!!

THE CAPTAIN ATTEMPTS TO SLOW DOWN IN ORDER TO FIGHT BETTER BUT SUDDENLY REALISES THAT HE HAS LOST CONTROL OF HIS MACHINE. AFTER ONE LAST VAULT, THE TANKS SLAMS INTO A PYLON...

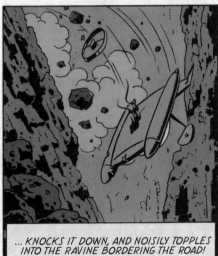

... KNOCKS IT DOWN, AND NOISILY TOPPLES INTO THE RAVINE BORDERING THE ROAD!

OUR UNFORTUNATE FRIEND IS THROWN INTO THE AIR THROUGH THE OPEN COCKPIT!

By Zeus! What a tumble!!!

He must be in bits!

FALLING, BLAKE REFLEXIVELY TURNS ON HIS PLANOS...

... AND IMMEDIATELY FINDS HIMSELF HOVERING 30 FEET OVER A FAST-FLOWING RIVER, AS IF SOME POWERFUL HAND HAD GRABBED HIM ON THE WAY DOWN. THE TANK, THOUGH, HITS THE WATER WITH A MIGHTY CRASH!

Just in time!

CASTING HIS GAZE ABOUT, THE CAPTAIN IS SURPRISED TO RECOGNISE THE VERY SPOT WHERE, A FEW HOURS BEFORE, HE AND HIS COMPANIONS HAD REACHED THE MAIN ROAD.

By Jove! This is the river that flows into the inner sea Icarus mentioned! All I have to do is follow the current!

WITHOUT HESITATION, HE FLIES OFF TOWARDS THE ONLY WAY TO POSEIDOPOLIS STILL OPEN TO HIM...

MEANWHILE, BACK IN BARBARIAN LANDS, ICARUS AND MORTIMER HAVE STARTED TOWARDS THE GREAT GATE ALONG THE PATH KNOWN ONLY TO THE PRINCE. BEFORE LEAVING THE COLLAPSED CRACK, THE YOUNG MAN HAS LEFT HIS NOW-USELESS PLANOS BEHIND, THE BETTER TO THROW THEIR PURSUERS OFF THE SCENT.

We'll have to cross a particularly dangerous jungle.

How so? Are there wild animals?

AT THAT MOMENT, THEY COME UPON A VAST SWAMP, AND THE PRINCE SIMPLY ANSWERS:

Worse than that. Look!

Goodness! Could it be true!? A Paleozoic forest!

A FANTASTIC FOREST STRETCHES BEFORE THE TWO MEN, MADE OF ENORMOUS, STRANGE-LOOKING PLANTS THAT SEEM PECULIARLY ANIMATED...

Well, let's go!

Watch yourself! Don't leave the trail! Almost all of those plants are carnivorous, and they're always ready to capture prey!

Understood.

CAREFULLY, ICARUS STARTS DOWN A SORT OF SLIPPERY TRAIL THAT SNAKES THROUGH THE EERIE JUNGLE, WHERE MONSTROUS INSECTS FLY, CRAWL, AND SLITHER...

THEY HAVE BEEN WALKING THUS FOR A GOOD WHILE WHEN MORTIMER, DRIVEN MAD BY THE HARASSING ATTENTIONS OF GIANT MOSQUITOES, MAKES A WILD GESTURE TO CHASE THEM AWAY AND DROPS HIS DISINTEGRATOR...

?

These accursed bugs!

... WHICH ROLLS INTO A MESS OF PLANTS. WITHOUT THINKING, HE LEAPS FORWARD TO PICK IT UP.

Stop, you fool!

TOO LATE! FAST AS A STRIKING SNAKE, A LONG, FLEXIBLE TENTACLE SWOOPS DOWN ON MORTIMER...

?

... AND LIFTS HIM LIKE A FEATHER!

HELP!!!

44

THE UNFORTUNATE MORTIMER HAS JUST BEEN CAPTURED BY A GIANT DROSERA, WHOSE STICKY TENTACLES ARE TIGHTLY WOUND AROUND HIM...

... AND ALREADY THE LEAVES ARE CLOSING AROUND THEIR CATCH. BUT ICARUS, WASTING NO TIME, FIRES HIS WEAPON AT THE CARNIVOROUS PLANT...

... CAUSING IT TO RELEASE MORTIMER STRAIGHTAWAY. THE PROFESSOR BEGINS SLIDING DOWN THE LIMB, BUT A NEIGHBOURING DROSERA GRABS HIS PLANOS AND PULLS HIM TOWARDS ITSELF...

ICARUS, SEEING THIS NEW DANGER, YELLS:

Leave your planos! Hurry!!!

WITH ONE MIGHTY EFFORT, MORTIMER TRIGGERS THE OPENING MECHANISM...

... AND FALLS HEAVILY TO THE GROUND.

BUT THE IMPACT IS SO SEVERE THAT HE REMAINS STILL. AS MENACING LIMBS SWOOP DOWN TOWARDS HIS COMPANION, THE PRINCE'S REFLEXES PROPEL HIM FORWARD...

Professor!!!

... BUT HE FAILS TO SEE, SPREAD OPEN ON THE GROUND, AN ENORMOUS VENUS FLYTRAP LYING IN AMBUSH!

HE HAS NO SOONER PUT HIS FOOT DOWN ONTO IT THAN IT SNAPS SHUT, TRAPPING THE UNFORTUNATE FELLOW...

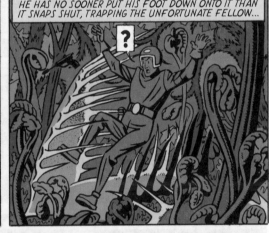

DESPITE HIS DESPERATE EFFORTS, AND BEGINNING TO SUFFOCATE, THE PRINCE IS UNABLE TO BREAK FREE OF THE TERRIBLE TRAP!

Help! Mortimer, Help!!!

THE SCREAMS ARE ENOUGH TO MAKE A STILL-DAZED MORTIMER SIT UP PAINFULLY...

What? What's going...?

UNDERSTANDING INSTANTLY THE HORRIBLE FATE THREATENING ICARUS, HE LEAPS TO HIS FEET AND RUSHES TOWARDS THE DEADLY PLANT.

Heavens! I've lost my pistol!

DISREGARDING THE DANGER TO HIMSELF, MORTIMER PUTS ALL HIS STRENGTH INTO TRYING TO LOOSEN THE THING'S HOLD. BUT ITS GRIP ONLY TIGHTENS.

I can't do it!!... I need an axe for this!

NEAR PANIC, MORTIMER FEVERISHLY CASTS ABOUT FOR SOMETHING TO USE WHEN HIS GAZE ALIGHTS ON A WIDE, FLAT STONE STUCK IN THE TRAIL'S EMBANKMENT...

Ah! There!

... HE GRABS IT AND, WITH A STRENGTH BORN OF DESPAIR, BEGINS HACKING AWAY AT THE PLANT'S LEAFSTALK UNTIL HE FINALLY SEVERS IT.

Got it!!!

A VISCOUS SUBSTANCE OOZES FROM THE CUT, AND THE DEADLY LOBES PULL APART, FREEING THEIR PRISONER.

Thank goodness he's alive!!!

I'm wrecked!!

MORTIMER HURRIES TO PULL HIS COMPANION ONTO THE TRAIL, DUBIOUS REFUGE IN THE MIDDLE OF THE CARNIVOROUS JUNGLE...

What a nightmare!!

SOON, THEIR COMPOSURE REGAINED, THE TWO FRIENDS TAKE STOCK...

What can we do now? No weapons and the planos is gone! No point in getting to that canyon under these conditions... We don't have the means to cross it!

True. Let's try to get to the Colossal Head instead. We'll figure out what we want to do there...

MAKING THEIR WAY THROUGH THE LETHAL MAZE, THE TWO MEN HAVE BEEN WALKING FOR SOME TIME WHEN, AS THEY FIND THEMSELVES ALONGSIDE A WIDE MARSHY AREA, THEY SUDDENLY HEAR A STRANGE SOUND.

Did you hear that?!...

It seems to be coming from the right!

ADVANCING CAUTIOUSLY THROUGH THE VEGETATION BORDERING THE PATH, THEY PEER ACROSS THE MARSH AND SEE A BARBARIAN STRUGGLING TO STAY AFLOAT...

Heavens!

A barbarian? Here!?...

HAVING CAUGHT SIGHT OF OUR FRIENDS, THE UNFORTUNATE MAN URGENTLY CALLS OUT TO BEG THEM...

Mercy, my lords! Help me!... And I swear, by Hunab Ku, I will forever be your faithful slave!!!

WITHIN SECONDS, ICARUS HAS HIS BELT UNDONE AND, WITH MORTIMER'S ASSISTANCE...

He swore... Besides, we can't let him die like this...

Yes, let's get him out of there!

... HE THROWS IT TO THE POOR WRETCH WHO GRABS ONTO IT...

Catch!

HE IS QUICKLY PULLED OUT OF THE MUD...

Hold on!

... AND COLLAPSES, EXHAUSTED, AS SOON AS HE REACHES SOLID GROUND...

Who are you? And what were you doing in this place your people fear so much?

I will tell you, Lord!

My name is Kisin, and I was part of the party sent to look for you under the orders of the surface lord. When we reached the Forbidden Forest, the men refused to enter it, citing the gods' orders. But the surfacer flew into a terrible rage and, under threat of the worst torture, he ordered my brother and me and two other warriors to explore this accursed place. Two of our companions were crushed by the serpent-tree, and it was while I attempted to save my poor brother from drowning that I, too, fell into the swamp... Oh! A thousand curses on the stranger! And blessed will be the time of my vengeance!!

Well, that time is near, as long as you obey me. Listen—this is what we have to do...

44

WHILE ICARUS AND MORTIMER ARE HAVING THEIR DANGEROUS ADVENTURES, BLAKE KEEPS FLYING TOWARDS THE INNER SEA.

SUDDENLY, GOING AROUND A BEND OF THE CLIFF, HE MAKES OUT THE VARIOUS BUILDINGS OF A SURVEILLANCE OUTPOST HUDDLED ON THE SHORE, THE LIGHTHOUSE FLASHING ITS RED EYE AT HIM EVERY FEW SECONDS.

Everything seems quiet...

HAVING OPTED FOR A MORE PRUDENT APPROACH ON FOOT, BLAKE CREEPS FROM ROCK TO ROCK UNTIL HE REACHES THE OUTPOST.

I wonder if this place is already under rebel control?...

EVERY SENSE FULLY ALERT, HE SNEAKS AROUND A BUILDING. ASIDE FROM THE DRONING OF THE RADARS, THOUGH, EVERYTHING IS SILENT.

Let's see what's inside here...

HOISTING HIMSELF UP TO THE WINDOW, HE GAZES THROUGH THE PLASTIC PANE AND SEES A ROOM FILLED WITH FOODSTUFFS.

Ho! Ho! That's a stroke of luck. I'm absolutely starving!

CATCHING SIGHT OF AN OPEN WINDOW A BIT FURTHER AWAY, HE IS SOON BREAKING INTO THE BUILDING.

Here we go!

CRATES AND BALES LINE THE DARK ROOM...

By Jove! Baskets of dried fruit—what a great find!

BUT, AS HE MAKES HIS WAY INSIDE, HE UNKNOWINGLY CUTS THE INVISIBLE RAY OF A PHOTOELECTRIC CELL, TRIGGERING THE ALARM...

INSTANTANEOUSLY, THE LIGHTS COME ON, BLINDINGLY BRIGHT...

DRRRRRRING

Damn!!!

... WHILE A DEAFENING RINGING FILLS THE WATCH ROOM WHERE THE SENTRY IS ON DUTY.

DRRRRRRRING

HE RUSHES TOWARDS THE ALARM BOARD...

It's in Block III!

... THEN, WITHOUT WASTING A MOMENT, RUNS OUTSIDE!

And the others are late coming back!...

MOMENTS LATER, HE BURSTS INTO THE WAREHOUSE, GUN IN HAND.

Who's there?!

BUT IT'S EMPTY.

No one!?! Wait, that open door there... I'll check the boathouse!

A FEW STEPS BRING HIM INTO THE NEXT ROOM. PUZZLED, HE STOPS...

Empty!... I'll be... Could it be a short circuit, or...

BUT A HARSH VOICE SUDDENLY ORDERS HIM:

Drop your weapon!!!

45

THE GUARD OBEYS. BLAKE, HAVING IDENTIFIED HIM AS ONE OF MAGON'S MEN THANKS TO HIS ARMBAND, CONTINUES:

All right, get down into that boat, and no funny business!

UNDERSTANDING THAT IT WOULD BE USELESS TO RESIST, THE MAN BOARDS THE BOAT RIGHT AWAY, FOLLOWED BY THE CAPTAIN.

Get behind the wheel!

And now, head straight for Poseidopolis!

THE ENGINE ROARS TO LIFE. THE CUTTER GLIDES ALONG THE QUAY, LEAVES THE HANGAR, THEN ACCELERATES...

...AND IS SOON SPEEDING AWAY FROM THE COAST AND INTO A STRONG SEA, HARBINGER OF HEAVY WEATHER...

AND THE STORM DOES NOT TAKE LONG TO ARRIVE! THE CLOUDS THAT WERE FLOATING OVER THE WAVES SUDDENLY TURN INK-BLACK, AND A MUFFLED RUMBLING ERUPTS FROM THE BOTTOM OF THE SEA...

AT THAT MOMENT, THE GUARD LETS OUT A JOYOUS CRY: LESS THAN A MILE AWAY, THE STRANGE SILHOUETTE OF A PATROL SHIP HAS JUST APPEARED...

ITS CAPTAIN, UPON CATCHING SIGHT OF THE CUTTER, IS BAFFLED...

That's Hadad! He left his post? Whatever for?...

With the storm that's coming? Is he insane?!

INTRIGUED, THE CAPTAIN ATTEMPTS TO CONTACT THE GUARD BY RADIO.

Hello, Hadad? What's going on? Where are you going?! Hadad!... Hadad!

BUT HADAD, ACUTELY AWARE OF THE GUN POINTING AT HIM, REMAINS SILENT.

Hadad! Are you deaf?!

Faster!!

Hmm... Something's not right here. Let's go after him... Full speed ahead!!

Full speed ahead!!

INCREASING ITS SPEED, THE PATROL SHIP FORCES ITS WAY THROUGH THE INCREASINGLY HIGH WAVES.

Faster!! Don't try to slow down!... If they catch up to us, my first bullet will be for you!

SEEING THEIR PURSUERS GAINING ON THEM, THE GUARD HATCHES A DESPERATE PLAN...

Faster!!!

AS THEY PASS NEAR A BUOY, HE SUDDENLY POINTS THE BOAT STRAIGHT AT IT. THEN, ESCAPING BLAKE'S VIGILANCE, HE DIVES INTO THE RAGING SEA!

TAKEN BY SURPRISE, THE CAPTAIN BARELY HAS TIME TO JUMP BEHIND THE WHEEL AND TURN HARD. THE CUTTER VEERS AWAY, SCRAPING THE BUOY, AND RESUMES ITS MAD RACE.

46

48

SWIMMING FOR HIS LIFE, HADAD HAS MANAGED TO GET A GRIP ON THE BUOY. THE PATROL SHIP STOPS TO RESCUE HIM.

Ahoy! Hold on!

AS SOON AS HE IS ABOARD, THE MAN RECOUNTS FOR THE CAPTAIN WHAT HE HAS BEEN THROUGH.

That's when I aimed the cutter at the buoy so it'd crash into it. But that bandit managed to avoid it...

There's no doubt: He's the surfacer we've been looking for in vain for hours... After him, flank speed!

AND THE SHIP RESUMES ITS RACE, ITS ENGINES PUSHED TO THEIR LIMITS. IT GAINS ON THE FUGITIVE QUICKLY, BUT NOW THE STORM'S FURY HAS REACHED ITS FULL FORCE. PEALS OF THUNDER ROLL WITHOUT INTERRUPTION, AND THE EVER-INCREASING DARKNESS IS CRISS-CROSSED BY BLINDING FLASHES OF LIGHTNING.

Curses! He's going to escape!... Ah, to Tartarus with him: Sink him!

THE PATROL SHIP'S DISINTEGRATOR BEGINS ROARING, CAUSING MASSIVE SPLASHES OF STEAM AND FOAM TO RISE...

BUT THE TOWERING WAVES HINDER THE SHOOTING DESPITE THE GUNNERS' EFFORTS.

Enough of this! Fire a...

THE ATLANTEAN CAPTAIN IS CUT OFF BY HADAD'S FRIGHTENED CRY...

Great Zeus! Look!!!

SUDDENLY, A CONICAL PROTUBERANCE EMERGES FROM A LOW CLOUD AND BEGINS SPINNING DOWN TOWARDS THE SEA, WHILE AT THE SAME TIME A MASS OF CHURNING WATER RISES TO MEET IT...

Watch it! A waterspout's forming!!!

INDEED, MOMENTS LATER THE TWO SECTIONS MEET, FORMING A COLUMN 200 YARDS IN DIAMETER. MOVING AT GREAT SPEED WITH AN APOCALYPTIC DIN, IT BEARS DOWN ON THE TWO SHIPS...

Full right rudder!!!

BLAKE, SEEING THIS NEW DANGER, ATTEMPTS TO ALTER HIS OWN BEARING.

Good heavens!

TOO LATE! MOVING AT OVER 500 MILES AN HOUR, THE MASSIVE COLUMN SMACKS INTO THE PATROL SHIP, FLINGING IT AWAY—WHERE IT LANDS IN PIECES!!

... AS FOR THE CUTTER, WHICH IS MORE MANOEUVRABLE, WHILE IT MANAGES TO STEER CLEAR OF THE COLUMN ITSELF, IT CANNOT AVOID THE WIND STORM THAT ACCOMPANIES IT. BLAKE IS SUCKED UP, TORN FROM HIS SEAT AND THROWN INTO THE VERY CENTRE OF THE WATERSPOUT...

FOR A SPLIT SECOND, HE PICTURES HIMSELF INSIDE A HUGE, EMPTY CYLINDER FILLED WITH LIGHT, WHILE AN INDESCRIBABLE ROARING PIERCES HIS EARDRUMS. THEN HE MERCIFULLY LOSES CONSCIOUSNESS...

47

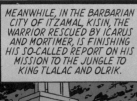

MEANWHILE, IN THE BARBARIAN CITY OF ITZAMAL, KISIN, THE WARRIOR RESCUED BY ICARUS AND MORTIMER, IS FINISHING HIS SO-CALLED REPORT ON HIS MISSION TO THE JUNGLE TO KING TLALAC AND OLRIK.

Are you certain of what you claim, then?

Absolutely, o great King! This was how I saw the two surfacers die, swallowed by the serpent-trees! And this helmet is the only thing that I could bring back.

Well, this is excellent news, o King! And a good omen for our endeavour!... I say you should offer this brave man a reward for his courage.

You're right! Let him be from now on the captain of my personal guard!

Praise be to you, o great King!

And now, my friends, the time has come! Let us go and watch the sacred dance that will be the prelude to our victory over the hated Atlanteans!

WHEN TLALAC, FOLLOWED BY OLRIK, APPEARS ON THE PALACE'S TERRACE, A TREMENDOUS ROAR RISES FROM THE CROWD.

Hail, Tlalac!

Hail, Tlalac!

Hail, Tlalac!

SATISFIED BY THIS RECEPTION, THE KING RAISES HIS HAND, AND SILENCE FALLS AT ONCE.

Warriors! Tomorrow at this time, you will march through the smoking ruins of prideful Poseidopolis!... The mighty god Hurakan will walk before you! His invincible power will turn the weapons and the walls of our enemies to dust! Therefore, to call upon us his favour and his magnanimous protection, you will dance for him and sing his glory!

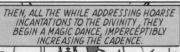

GREAT WAR DRUMS BEGIN TO BOOM TO AN INSISTENT RHYTHM AS FOUR SHAMANS, WEARING GHASTLY MASKS, JUMP ONTO THE TEMPLE SQUARE...

BEGINNING A STRANGE CHANT, THEY STEP CLOSER TO THE FIRE THAT BURNS AT THE FOOT OF THE STATUE OF HURAKAN. AFTER THEY LAY THEIR HANDS ON IT, BRIGHT FLAMES SUDDENLY SPRING HIGH INTO THE SKY...

THEN, ALL THE WHILE ADDRESSING HOARSE INCANTATIONS TO THE DIVINITY, THEY BEGIN A MAGIC DANCE, IMPERCEPTIBLY INCREASING THE CADENCE.

MESMERISED BY THE STRANGE SPECTACLE, THE WARRIORS JOIN IN, ONE AFTER ANOTHER. SOON, COMPLETELY ENTRANCED, THE ENTIRE PEOPLE ENTER THE CIRCLE, WHICH TWISTS AND SWAYS TO THE FURIOUS RUMBLE OF THE DRUMS...

BUT EVEN AS THIS COLLECTIVE FRENZY IS REACHING ITS CLIMAX, NO ONE NOTICES THE NEW CAPTAIN OF THE ROYAL GUARD SLIPPING AWAY DISCREETLY...

48

MAKING HIS WAY QUICKLY THROUGH THE DESERTED SQUARES AND PLATFORMS OF THE PALACE, KISIN SOON REACHES THE CITY'S OUTER WALL. LEANING OVER THE MOAT, HE UTTERS A PECULIAR CALL...

Hooyoohoo!

... WHICH ICARUS'S VOICE IMMEDIATELY ANSWERS. PULLING A LONG KNOTTED ROPE FROM UNDER A ROCK, THE WARRIOR THROWS IT DOWN. STRONG HANDS GRAB IT, AND...

... MOMENTS LATER, THE PRINCE AND MORTIMER CLIMB OVER THE PARAPET.

Everything is fine, Lords. I was made captain of the guard, and I know what to do so you can get back to Atlantis. Quick, now, follow me to the temple! The celebrations are underway, and we must be there before the shamans return.

Lead on...

SOON, HAVING PUT THE GENERAL INATTENTION TO GOOD USE, THE THREE MEN ARRIVE SAFELY AT A CONCEALED DOOR AND SNEAK INSIDE THE TEMPLE OF HURAKAN.

The cells are at the very end of the gallery. Come!...

AT THAT SAME MOMENT, 100 MILES FROM ITZAMAL, BLAKE, WHO HAS BEEN DROPPED BY THE WATERSPOUT FAR FROM WHERE HE STARTED AND HAS ONLY SURVIVED THANKS TO HIS WATERPROOF EQUIPMENT, PAINFULLY COMES TO HIS SENSES ON AN EMPTY BEACH...

Heavens! That was too close for comfort... But which way am I to go now?

THE CAPTAIN STUMBLES TO HIS FEET AND, UNSTEADY STEP AFTER UNSTEADY STEP, HEADS TOWARDS A ROCKY RIDGE...

From there I might be able to get my bearings...

NO SOONER HAS HE GAZED UPON THE HORIZON, THOUGH, THAN HE EXCLAIMS WITH STUPEFACTION:

The devil?! Am I going mad?! That lighthouse... those buildings... Could it be?

THE PLACE HE SEES IN THE DISTANCE IS NONE OTHER THAN THE SMALL COASTAL OUTPOST HE LEFT TWO HOURS EARLIER! INSTEAD OF CARRYING HIM TOWARDS THE CAPITAL, THE STORM HAS BROUGHT HIM BACK TO WHERE HE STARTED!

Damn! I must leave this place right away!...

TOO LATE! STUNNED BY THE SITUATION, BLAKE HAS NOT NOTICED A NAVY SPHEROS THAT HAS STOPPED IN MIDAIR, ALLOWING ITS OCCUPANTS TO LOOK AT HIM CLOSELY...

By Zeus! That's our man!

Go!

BEFORE BLAKE HAS A CHANCE TO REALISE THE DANGER HE IS IN, THE SPHEROS IS BARRING HIS WAY AND THREE ARMBAND-WEARING GUARDS OVERPOWER HIM...

We've got you, surfacer!

... BEFORE THROWING HIM INTO THE CRAFT...

Mission accomplished! Let's go. And make sure nothing happens to him: Magon wants him alive!

Yes, Archon.

TIME PASSES... THE TIME OF THE GREAT BARBARIAN INVASION HAS COME. FOLLOWING ITS SHAMANS, THE HUGE ARMY HAS BEGUN ITS MARCH; NOW, THE VANGUARD, LED BY OLRIK, IS CROSSING THE ROPE BRIDGE OVER THE GREAT CHASM, WHILE THE MAIN BODY OF TROOPS IS MASSING BEFORE THE GREAT GATE, WAITING TO SET FOOT ONTO ATLANTEAN SOIL AFTER SO MANY CENTURIES OF INVIOLABILITY!!!

HAVING PASSED THAT FIRST OBSTACLE, THE ARMY MARCHES INTO ARROW PASS. IN THE FRONT ROW IS LOYAL KISIN, THE NEW CAPTAIN OF THE ROYAL GUARD. BEHIND HIM, RESTING ON HIS PALANQUIN, OLRIK GAZES AT THE FOUR SHAMANS WHO DANCE AND MIME THE INCANTATIONS THAT WILL CLEAR THE WARRIORS' PATH OF EVIL SPIRITS.

NO ONE SUSPECTS THAT TWO OF THE SHAMANS ARE NONE OTHER THAN MORTIMER AND THE PRINCE...

So? How much longer must we continue with this monkey business?

Patience! We'll try to slip away when we reach the Gong Tower...

... WHO, WITH THE HELP OF KISIN, MANAGED TO AMBUSH THE REAL SHAMANS IN THEIR CELLS AND DON THEIR ATTIRE!... THE TOWER IS SOON IN SIGHT, AND ICARUS GIVES THE CAPTAIN A DISCREET SIGNAL. KISIN IMMEDIATELY ORDERS HIS TROOPS TO STOP, LETTING THE SHAMANS CONTINUE ALONE TOWARDS THE BRIDGE THAT LEADS TO THE FORTRESS AND ITS TWO PHULOS ON GUARD DUTY.

Well? What's going on?!

Our shamans are going to purify this place before our men go near it, Lord!

Do you see the spheros in the courtyard?

Zeus is with us! Smartly, now! Do exactly as I do!...

MIMICKED BY THE PROFESSOR, ICARUS DANCES TOWARDS THE SURPRISED GUARDS WITH MUCH ENTHUSIASTIC GESTURING, AND THEN...

... THROWING AWAY THEIR UNWIELDY MASKS, THE TWO MEN SPRINT TOWARDS THE ENTRANCE.

Let's go!!!

ALAS! MORTIMER HAS GONE NO MORE THAN 10 YARDS WHEN, CATCHING HIS FEET IN HIS LONG CLOAK, HE FALLS HEAVILY TO THE GROUND.

Ow!

AT THAT SIGHT, OLRIK LETS OUT A ROAR OF OUTRAGE!

Mortimer and the prince!? By the devil! Fire!... Fire, you imbeciles!!!

SEEING THE DANGER, THOUGH, KISIN HAS LEAPT FORWARD. AND BEFORE THE TWO STUNNED PHULOS HAD A CHANCE OF EVEN PULLING OUT THEIR WEAPONS, HE KNOCKS THEM OUT WITH TWO BLOWS OF HIS TERRIBLE MACE!!!

THEN HE TURNS TO FACE OLRIK, ATTEMPTING TO COVER HIS FRIENDS' ESCAPE. BUT THE COLONEL HAS HIS WHOLE ESCORT WITH HIM. THE FIGHT IS TOO UNEQUAL, AND SOON...

Haa!...

Traitor!

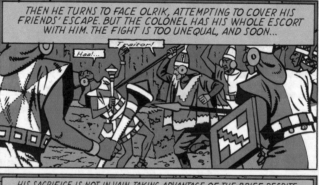

HIS SACRIFICE IS NOT IN VAIN. TAKING ADVANTAGE OF THE BRIEF RESPITE, ICARUS HAS MANAGED TO DRAG A STILL-DAZED MORTIMER INTO THE COURTYARD. UNFORTUNATELY, JUST AS THEY ARE ABOUT TO REACH THE SPHEROS, TWO MORE GUARDS APPEAR BEFORE THEM...

Halt!

Too late! Quick, to the tower!!!

FRANTICALLY SCRAMBLING UP STAIRS AND RUBBLE, THEY HEAD TOWARDS THE COMMANDER'S CHAMBER, WHERE THE WEAPONS DESTINED FOR THE UPRISING ARE STOCKPILED...

Hurry! If we can reach the weapons cache, we're saved!

BUT EVEN AS THEY ENTER THE COMMANDER'S QUARTERS, THEY FIND A GUARD WAITING FOR THEM, WEAPON IN HAND...

Ha! Ha! I've got you, you rats!!!

THE REBEL HAS NO TIME FOR FURTHER WORDS, THOUGH, FOR A MAN DROPS HEAVILY ONTO HIM FROM THE TOP OF THE STAIRCASE!

Ow!

FLABBERGASTED, ICARUS AND MORTIMER RECOGNISE THEIR FRIEND IN THIS PROVIDENTIAL SAVIOUR...

Blake!!!

You! Here?! But how!?!

Later!... Just know that I was being held prisoner up there in the watch room and that when this ruffian here went to take care of you, I... took care of him!

THE ANGRY SHOUTS OF THEIR PURSUERS RISE FROM THE LOWER LEVEL...

Well done, Captain! But here they come! Let's arm ourselves with their weapons!

Too late! The phulos took them away...

Oh, no!... It's over, then. Our mission is a failure. My people will not be alerted in time. Atlantis is lost!!!

BUT MORTIMER EXCLAIMS...

No! We have one last card to play: the Sacred Gong!

The gong!?! Great Zeus, I forgot!

Well thought, old boy! You go; we'll hold them back here!

You can count on me! We'll see if the legend is true!

Go! And strike hard!

WHILE HIS COMPANIONS KEEP THE ENEMY'S HEAD DOWN, MORTIMER DASHES OFF... BUT, ONCE ON THE TERRACE, HE SUDDENLY COMES FACE TO FACE WITH OLRIK WHO, CUNNING AS EVER, IS LEADING A SECONDARY ASSAULT FROM THE OUTSIDE...

Hell!!?!

Ha! This time, I've got you!

TOO EARLY! RECOVERING FROM THE SHOCK ON THE SPOT, MORTIMER PLANTS A FORMIDABLE LEFT HOOK ON HIS ADVERSARY'S JAW...

Not yet!

Oomph!

...THEN, HAVING TORN HIS MACE OUT OF HIS HAND, HE TURNS HIS FURY TOWARDS THE BARBARIANS, PUSHING THEM BACK TO THE PARAPET... THEN OVER IT...

...BEFORE SHOVING THEIR LADDER OFF THE WALL!

WITHOUT WASTING ANOTHER MOMENT, HE RUSHES UP THE STAIRS.

BREATHING HARD, HE STOPS AT THE FOOT OF THE ENORMOUS GONG. MUSTERING ALL HIS STRENGTH, HE PREPARES TO STRIKE IT, BUT...

... CANNOT FINISH THE MOVEMENT: A JAVELIN, THROWN BY OLRIK, WHISTLES THROUGH THE AIR AND TEARS THE MACE OUT OF HIS HAND!...

THE VILLAIN, THOUGH STILL DIZZY, HAS GUESSED THE PROFESSOR'S INTENTION AND STUMBLED AFTER HIM. SEEING HIS SHOT GONE WILD, IF LUCKILY SO, HE CHARGES HIS UNARMED OPPONENT, HIS OWN WEAPON HELD HIGH...

This is the end of you!

MORTIMER, THOUGH, KEEPS HIS WITS ABOUT HIM, DODGES THE BLOW, AND HURLS HIMSELF AT HIS OPPONENT. GETTING A GOOD HOLD ON HIM...

... HE DIGS UP RESERVES OF IRRESISTIBLE STRENGTH, LIFTS HIM BODILY...

BUT THE CENTURIES-OLD ROPES FINALLY GIVE WAY, AND THE COLOSSAL BRONZE DISK SLAMS HEAVILY ONTO THE PLATFORM, WOBBLES A MOMENT...

BONG

... AND THEN, WITH A SERIES OF THUNDEROUS CRASHES THAT THE ECHO INCREASES EXPONENTIALLY, ROLLS OFF THE EDGE, BOUNCING DOWN TIER AFTER TIER AND CRUSHING EVERYTHING IN ITS PATH. BEHIND IT, A DEADLY RAIN OF ROCKS, SHAKEN LOOSE BY THE VIBRATIONS, FALLS FROM THE CEILING AND SPREADS PANIC AND TERROR AMONG THE BARBARIANS...

BONG

BONG

... AND THROWS HIM HARD ONTO THE GONG, CAUSING AN EXTRAORDINARY RUMBLING TO RISE AND ECHO FROM THE OLD WALLS FOR A LONG TIME...

BONG

WASTING NO TIME, MORTIMER RACES DOWN FROM THE UPPER LEVEL TO JOIN HIS FRIENDS, WHOSE ENEMIES, STRICKEN BY THE SAME PANIC, HAVE ALSO FLED.

The coast is clear!! Let's go!!!

Hurray!

To the spheros!

FROM THE GOVERNOR'S CHAMBER, THE THREE MEN REACH THE COURTYARD IN THREE SHAKES AND, IN THE GENERAL PANIC, RUSH TO THE ABANDONED CRAFT...

Quick!

... PILE IN, AND TAKE OFF IN A SINGLE MOVE, PEPPERED BY A STORM OF IMPOTENT ARROWS AND CHASED BY OLRIK'S CURSES...

You'll pay for this!

54

WHILE THESE DRAMATIC EVENTS TAKE PLACE, THE POWERFUL SOUNDS OF THE SACRED GONG HAVE RAISED THE ALARM IN POSEIDOPOLIS, CAUSING ASTONISHMENT AND CONSTERNATION. MAGON, SURPRISED BY THIS UNEXPECTED TURN OF EVENTS, HAS RUSHED TO THE BASILEUS'S SIDE IN AN ATTEMPT TO DOWNPLAY THE FACTS...

There's no doubt in my mind, Your Majesty. The gong must have fallen after the ropes holding it snapped, and...

That's possible. But I still called Omegara. I want to know!

SOON, PHOKIS, THE OUTPOST COMMANDER, APPEARS ON THE SCREEN.

Well, Phokis? What's going on?

I don't know, Your Majesty. I was about to send a patrol to go check at the... Ah! I'm told there's a spheros coming our way!

IT IS THE VEHICLE OUR THREE FRIENDS USED TO ESCAPE THAT HAS JUST COME INTO VIEW OF THE FORT. AND...

Sound the alarm! The barbarians are attacking! We've been betrayed!!

Betrayed!?

SHOCKED, THE COMMANDER REAPPEARS AND RESUMES HIS REPORT.

Your Majesty!... Dire news, Your Majesty! The barbarians have breached the Great Gate!!! We've been

!

?

BUT, AT THAT VERY MOMENT A BOLT OF FIRE STRIKES NEAR THE TRANSMISSION TOWER, DESTROYING THE ANTENNAS...

THE SCREEN INSTANTLY BLANKS OUT. IN THE SUDDEN SILENCE, THE STUNNED VIEWERS ARE LEFT TO THEIR DISBELIEF...

Phokis is mad! I cannot believe that...

Enough!... Muster the troops, and call a meeting of the Council within the hour. Go!...

BACK AT OMEGARA, THE SITUATION IS QUICKLY WORSENING. PHOKIS, UNDERSTANDING THAT THE WISEST COURSE IS TO FALL BACK TO THE CAPITAL RIGHT AWAY, ORDERS THE EVACUATION.

Hello! Hello! The entire garrison must board the monorail immediately! Hurry up!!!

DESPITE THE SUSTAINED FIRE FROM THEIR INVISIBLE ENEMY, THE OUTPOST'S MEN OBEY THEIR ORDERS WITH SPEED AND DISCIPLINE.

THE MONORAIL FINALLY LEAVES JUST AS THE ARMOURY IS HIT AND GOES UP IN A SPECTACULAR EXPLOSION!...

UNFORTUNATELY, THIS IS NOT THE END OF IT. FROM THE AIR WHERE THEY ARE ESCORTING THE CONVOY, OUR FRIENDS CAN CLEARLY SEE THAT THE TRAIN IS ADVANCING IN THE MIDDLE OF A CIRCLE OF EXPLOSIONS THAT TRAVELS WITH IT AND SLOWLY TIGHTENS...

I doubt they'll be able to make it... Those things are nasty...

And there's nothing we can do to help!

NO SOONER HAVE THEY UTTERED THESE WORDS THAN THE MONORAIL IS STRUCK DEAD-ON AND BLOWN TO SMITHEREENS!

CAUGHT IN THE SHOCKWAVE, THE SPHEROS TIPS OVER IN THE AIR AND BEGINS TUMBLING DOWN TOWARDS THE GROUND, DESPITE ICARUS'S DESPERATE EFFORTS TO PULL UP...

GRIPPING THE CONTROLS WITH ALL HIS STRENGTH, THE PRINCE SUCCEEDS IN SLOWING THE SPHEROS'S FALL, AND THE CRIPPLED CRAFT'S CONTACT WITH THE GROUND IS MERELY BRUTAL. IT BEGINS TO ROLL DOWN A SLOPE...

... BUT A MIRACLE SEES ONE OF THE LANDING STRUTS CATCH ONTO A ROCKY OUTCROPPING, AND THE SPHEROS COMES TO REST ON THE EDGE OF A DEEP CHASM.

THE PASSENGERS, WHO HAVE BEEN ROUGHLY THROWN ABOUT INSIDE THE VEHICLE, PAINFULLY CRAWL OUT OF THE WRECK...

Good grief! That was a close one!

No broken bones?

No, I'm fine!

This is all very well, but it's not getting us any closer to Poseidopolis!

True enough! Listen. We have one last possibility. Not too far from here is another monorail line. Maybe there, we can find another means to travel.

Let's go!

AFTER A SHORT BUT DIFFICULT WALK THROUGH THE WILD AND BARREN COUNTRY, OUR THREE FRIENDS REACH THE LINE, ON WHICH CONVOY AFTER CONVOY OF BARBARIAN TROOPS ARE HEADING TOWARDS THE CAPITAL.

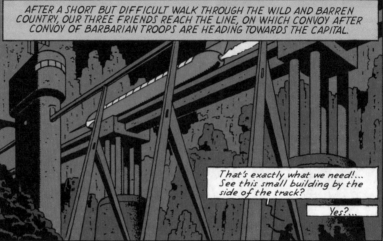

That's exactly what we need!... See this small building by the side of the track?

Yes?...

It's one of the many posts that are built along the line and ensure the safety of all traffic. It's stocked with lenses and spare parts, but there's also a "celeros" kept there—a small, fast vehicle used for inspecting tracks. But we must take care that it's not being guarded!

WITH INFINITE CAUTION, THEY SNEAK TO THE DEPOT. FORTUNATELY, IT TURNS OUT TO BE DESERTED.

Careful! We can't be seen by a convoy!

THEY HURRY TO THE DOOR, AND ICARUS QUICKLY EXAMINES THE OPENING MECHANISM.

If they haven't changed the combination, we're...

IT ONLY TAKES THE LIGHTEST TOUCH OF HIS HAND, THOUGH, TO OPEN THE DOOR AND TURN ON THE LIGHTS.

By Zeus! What a stroke of luck! Clothes, weapons!!

It must be a rebel cache...

Good! I can't wait to take these rags off!

A FEW MINUTES LATER, FULLY EQUIPPED AND ARMED, OUR THREE FRIENDS ARE READY TO ACT...

Ah! I feel like a new man! Being a shaman was definitely not for a scientist like me!

This way, quick! Staying here any longer would be a mistake...

We're right behind you!!

THE PRINCE LEADS THEM THROUGH A DOOR AND INTO A HANGAR, WHERE A STOUT VEHICLE WITH TWO POWERFUL SEARCHLIGHTS IS WAITING ON ITS RAIL...

Let's get in! We must slip in between two convoys, and the last one just went by a second ago...

All right!

THEN, HAVING BOARDED THE CELEROS AND MADE SURE THAT NO OTHER CONVOY IS IN SIGHT, OUR HEROES SPEED OFF TOWARDS THE MAIN LINE, AT THE END OF WHICH THEY WILL FIND... THE BATTLE!

WHILE THE THREE MEN BARREL DOWN TOWARDS POSEIDOPOLIS, THE CAPITAL CITY—HALF OF IT ALREADY IN THE HANDS OF THE INVADERS—IS FIGHTING A DESPERATE BATTLE AGAINST THE BARBARIAN HORDE, WHICH, THANKS TO THE TREACHERY OF MAGON AND HIS ACCOMPLICES, IS SWEEPING AWAY EVERYTHING IN ITS PATH. SABOTAGED, THE ATLANTEAN BATTERIES ARE OVERRUN ONE BY ONE, THEIR CREWS SLAUGHTERED ON THE SPOT...

Run away!

By Zeus! What are you waiting for? Fire!!!

I can't! The firing mechanism is jammed!!!

Hello! Hello! This is Archias battery; the guns have been sabotaged!

SEEING THE SCOPE AND SERIOUSNESS OF THE SITUATION, THE BASILEUS HAS ORDERED ALL SURVIVORS TO TAKE REFUGE INSIDE THE IMPREGNABLE FORTRESS THAT IS THE ROYAL PALACE...

Why don't we use air power to exterminate that scum?...

We can't without hitting our own people!!! They're inside our lines!

... WHILE, IN THE COMMAND CHAMBER, AMIDST THE BAD NEWS THAT KEEPS COMING, THE OVERWHELMED STAFF TRIES IN VAIN TO STOP THE ENEMY'S ADVANCE...

Hello! Hello! This is the Ogygia sector CP! The second line is breached! Awaiting orders...

Hello! Hello! This is the Kylokastron... Captain Archias orders: Break contact and fall back to block 12! Hello! Hello!...

Hello! Hello! Calling Kylos air terminal! Hello! Hello!

Hello!... Orders for Pirgos battery: Hold your position at all costs!...

Hello! Hello! This is the Kylokastron!

Hello! Hello!

BUT THE COORDINATED ACTIONS OF THE REBELS SPREAD THROUGHOUT THE RANKS OF THE ATLANTEANS CAUSE THE KEY DEFENSIVE POSITIONS TO FALL TO THE ENEMY, ONE BY ONE.

Go on, Archon! Surrender if you value your life!!!

Hands up!

Traitor!!!

BUT, AS GUARDS AND BARBARIANS FIGHT BITTER HAND-TO-HAND BATTLES THROUGHOUT THE STREETS, ICARUS, BLAKE, AND MORTIMER ARE RUNNING THROUGH THE RUINS OF THE BURNING CITY, HEADING TOWARDS THE PALACE.

Almost there! The entrance to the underground passages is very near!

I hope we get there in time!...

Hello! Hello! This is Merope sector!... The great dam has fallen! Awaiting orders!...

EVENTS ARE STILL UNROLLING AT BREAKNECK SPEED, THOUGH. SUDDENLY, EVERY VIEWSCREEN SHUTS OFF AT THE SAME TIME, DISABLING ALL COMMUNICATIONS, AND A WOUNDED OFFICER STUMBLES INTO THE ROOM...

Your Majesty! The television station has been destroyed! Sabotage!!!

How can it be?

Here?

Sabotage!

Hello! Hello! This is the Melkart sector CP... The spheros station has been taken by the barbarians! Awaiting orders!...

STUNNED BY HOW SWIFT AND COMPLETE THE DISASTER IS, THE BASILEUS PRESSES MAGON HARD. THE CONTARKOS TRIES HIS BEST TO ALLAY THE SUSPICIONS THAT HANG OVER HIM...

Phokis is right! It's impossible that our strongest defences would fall without a fight like this; there's something afoot here...

Your Majesty! These are no more than unfortunate coincidences... Besides, who could even consider helping the barbarians!?

My friends! This latest blow could paralyse our defences. Extreme measures are required. We must steel ourselves and use our deadliest weapons...

AT THAT MOMENT, MAGON'S VOICE, BITING AND HARSH, RISES LIKE A CHALLENGE.

Too late, Basileus!!!

55

MAGON'S SHOCKING INTERVENTION HAS MUCH THE SAME EFFECT AS LIGHTNING STRIKING THE ROOM, AND THE ASSEMBLED AIDES, DUMBFOUNDED, FALL SILENT. EVENTUALLY, THE BASILEUS FINDS HIS VOICE...

What do you mean?

I mean, o Basileus, that your reign is at an end!

Know that my actions and those of my loyal followers have had but one goal: to make it easy for King Tlalac and his warriors to shatter your defences. They've already entered the palace... As a matter of fact, here they are!

INDEED, THE DOOR OPENS WITH A LOUD BANG ON THEODOS, GUIDING TLALAC, OLRIK, AND A MASS OF FIERCE BARBARIANS...

AS HE FINALLY UNDERSTANDS THE REASON BEHIND THE INCOMPREHENSIBLE DEFEAT OF THE ATLANTEANS, THE BASILEUS EXCLAIMS:

Now I understand why Icarus was so intent on that expedition to the edge of the empire... He couldn't believe that one of our own could be so treacherous and was looking for some proof to unmask you, you knave!!

Watch yourself, tyrant!... My men and I are tired of your termite kingdom and your insane dreams! You're defeated! As for your nephew and those surfacer dogs, they're dead!... I'm the ruler here now!!!

As for us, Basileus, we will make the surfacers up there feel the bite of our weapons. But my people and I have old scores to settle with your accursed race! The moment we've waited for so long is here at last... You will pay!!!

You miserable fools! Your pride will be your downfall!!!! You...

Enough talk! Seize him!

HOWEVER, A COMMANDING VOICE STOPS THE BARBARIANS IN THEIR TRACKS...

? Stop!

AT THE ENTRANCE OF THE COMMAND ROOM, BEHIND THE DOOR THAT HAS JUST OPENED, THE PRINCE, BLAKE, AND MORTIMER ARE NOW STANDING, WEAPONS IN HAND!

Praise be to Zeus!!! My nephew!

Yes, uncle! Back with these loyal friends through the secret passage known only to the royal family... and just in time, it seems!

OLRIK, SENSING THAT SWIFT ACTION IS NECESSARY, RAISES A DISINTEGRATOR HE HAS PICKED UP DURING THE INVASION, AND, AIMING FOR THE PRINCE, OPENS FIRE...

BUT MORTIMER IS FASTER THAN THE MISCREANT, AND, WITH A SUDDEN PUSH, HE SHOVES THE PRINCE OUT OF THE WAY. THE DISCHARGE STRIKES A LARGE MACHINE, WHICH EXPLODES WITH A DEAFENING BLAST...

BROM

THE SIGHT DRAWS A TERRIBLE CRY FROM THE BASILEUS...

By Tartarus!... He's just caused the gates that hold back the ocean to open!... Atlantis is doomed!!!

*

56

58

AT THIS TERRIFYING EXCLAMATION, EVERYONE IN THE ROOM FREEZES IN PLACE. A LOW RUMBLING SOUND, CAUSED BY THE WATERS RUSHING FREELY, SHAKES THE COLOSSAL WALLS OF THE PALACE AS IF TO PUNCTUATE THE BASILEUS'S CRY.

Listen!

No! The ocean!

Gates!?! What does he mean?

What is this?

BUT, TAKING ADVANTAGE OF THE CONFUSION, THE PRINCE DASHES TOWARDS THE COMMAND CONSOLE THAT CONTROLS AND MONITORS EVERY VITAL ORGAN OF THE UNDERGROUND CITY AND SWIFTLY PULLS DOWN ONE OF THE SWITCHES...

... CAUSING A BLINDING GATE OF FIRE TO COME DOWN FROM THE CEILING AND SLAM BETWEEN THE ATLANTEANS AND THEIR TERRIFIED ENEMIES...

! KRRRRAK

... WHO, PANIC-STRICKEN, RETREAT TOWARDS THE CORRIDOR IN DISARRAY, DRIVEN BACK BY THE STRANGE, MOVING WALL OF FLAME.

Huehueteotl's fire!!!

Damnation!!!

We're doomed!

AS FOR MAGON, FINDING HIMSELF CUT OFF FROM HIS ALLIES AND AT THE MERCY OF THE ONE HE HAS JUST BEEN THREATENING, HE THROWS HIMSELF AT THE FEET OF THE KING.

Mercy, Basileus!!!

Away, you wretch!... Let Poseidon alone decide your fate!!!

TURNING TOWARDS HIS LOYAL SUBJECTS, HE ADDS:

Follow me!

EVERYONE GOES AFTER HIM INTO THE COMMAND ROOM, WITHOUT EVEN SPARING A GLANCE FOR THE TRAITOR WHO SEES THE HEAVY DOOR SLAM SHUT IN HIS FACE...

? KLAK

REALISING AT LAST WHAT LIES IN WAIT FOR HIM, DRIVEN MAD BY FEAR, MAGON BEGINS HAMMERING ON THE CLOSED DOOR WITH HIS FISTS...

By almighty Zeus, don't leave me!!... Open, I beg you!! Mercy!

MEANWHILE, ON THE OTHER SIDE OF THE CITY, THE OCEAN, FREED BY THE DESTRUCTION OF THE CONTROL PULPIT, RUSHES IN, FLOODING THE ANCIENT DAM AND STORMING ATLANTIS!

THE BASILEUS, ICARUS, BLAKE, MORTIMER, AND THE OTHERS HAVE REACHED A VAST HALL WHERE THE SURVIVORS OF THE ATLANTEAN PEOPLE HAVE GATHERED...

SPEAKING SOLEMNLY, THE SOVEREIGN BEGINS ADDRESSING THEM:

My friends! Very grave events have just forced me to move forward the date we had set as the closing of our underground life. Magon the traitor, by opening our city to the barbarians, unwittingly severed the last tie we had with this world! Therefore, our scientists are going to take us away from our empire, once more swallowed by the sea, and lead us to the other side of the galaxy and a more hospitable planet! Everything is ready. Our interplanetary disks have long since explored and prepared our path... You will follow your leaders and board the interstellar ships that await you, and soon we will once again live free, under a triple sun billions of leagues from here...

HAVING SPOKEN THUS, THE BASILEUS WALKS TO A PULPIT AND VERY DELIBERATELY PUTS HIS FINGER ON A BUTTON...

IMMEDIATELY, THE ENTIRE BACK WALL OPENS SOUNDLESSLY, REVEALING AN ENORMOUS CAVE WHERE ENDLESS RANKS OF SPACESHIPS STRETCH INTO THE DISTANCE, SURROUNDED BY SUITED ASTRONAUTS.

Go, my friends. Go with order and discipline. Your trials are nearly over!...

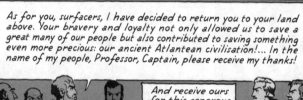

As for you, surfacers, I have decided to return you to your land above. Your bravery and loyalty not only allowed us to save a great many of our people but also contributed to saving something even more precious: our ancient Atlantean civilisation!... In the name of my people, Professor, Captain, please receive my thanks!

And receive ours for this generous gesture, o Basileus!

Icarus, take these good men to the place you know of and make sure they see the light of day again!... Go! Time is of the essence! Farewell, and a safe trip back to your world!

Farewell, Basileus. And may your endeavours succeed!

AND WHILE THE ATLANTEANS, FULL OF CONFIDENCE IN THE FUTURE, EMBARK TOWARDS THEIR NEW DESTINY, THE PRINCE HURRIEDLY LEADS BLAKE AND MORTIMER AWAY...

This way—come on!

MEANWHILE, OUTSIDE, THE OCEAN CONTINUES ITS WORK OF DEVASTATION, AND ITS UNSTOPPABLE WATERS HAVE ALREADY HALF-FLOODED THE CAPITAL CITY. CAUGHT INSIDE THE RAPIDLY FILLING PALACE, THE CURSED ARCHITECTS OF THE TERRIBLE DISASTER ARE STRUGGLING TO SAVE THEIR LIVES!

Help me, great Hurakan! Hear me! Your son Tlalac orders you to rescue him!...

Back! Away, ocean!... I am Magon, the basileus!... You will obey me!!!... Save me, guards!!!

Damnation!... Drowning like a rat!... Ah, I must keep looking!... Surely there must be a way out somewhere!?!...

LED BY ICARUS, THE TWO MEN REACH A THICK, REINFORCED HATCH.

This is the entrance to the lock where we keep the remote-controlled bathyscaphe that will take you home...

INDEED, A STRANGE-LOOKING VESSEL IS THERE, WAITING TO SUBMERGE AND LEAVE...

I will control the bathyscaphe myself...

My friends, the time has come to bid our farewells! But know that the best memory I shall take from this Earth is that of your loyal, unwavering friendship. Tell the men of the surface that they are on the verge of a new era full of marvellous possibilities, but that neither science nor victory by arms will ever bring them peace or true happiness as long as they don't purge their hearts of the twin plagues of hatred and stupidity!... May the disaster that befell Atlantis be a warning to them!...

SUDDENLY, A LONG, THREATENING RUMBLE CAUSES THE GROUND TO SHAKE BELOW THEIR FEET...

Hurry now! The dam just failed!!! Farewell, my friends!

Farewell!

God be with you, Prince!

AS THE PRINCE HAD GUESSED, ATLANTIS'S LAST DEFENCE HAS GIVEN WAY UNDER THE TREMENDOUS PRESSURE OF THE RAGING WATERS. AS THE WALLS OF THE CAVE CRACK AND BREAK EVERYWHERE, A MASSIVE WAVE SWEEPS THROUGH PROUD POSEIDOPOLIS...

AS FOR BLAKE AND MORTIMER, THEY FOLLOW ICARUS'S INSTRUCTIONS. THEY HAVE BARELY SET FOOT INSIDE THE SUBMERSIBLE WHEN THEY HEAR THE PRINCE'S VOICE COMING FROM A SPEAKER...

Take a seat and fasten your seatbelts! Tight!...

WITH THAT DONE, ICARUS OPENS THE SLUICES. THE LOCK FILLS QUICKLY, A STEEL GATE OPENS, AND SLOWLY THE CRAFT GETS UNDERWAY...

... MOMENTS LATER, HAVING NEGOTIATED A LONG TUNNEL CARVED THROUGH THE ROCK, THE BATHYSCAPHE COMES OUT INTO THE DARK OCEAN WATERS...

THAT IS WHEN A VIEW HOLE OPENS IN FRONT OF THE TWO MEN, JUST AS POWERFUL SEARCHLIGHTS ARE TURNED ON...

OH!

59

61

This is all that's left of ancient Atlantis, destroyed by the sea over 10,000 years ago!

ICARUS'S VOICE ANSWERS BLAKE AND MORTIMER'S AMAZED EXCLAMATION AT THE INCREDIBLE AND GRANDIOSE SIGHT UNFOLDING BEFORE THEM: THE SUNKEN RUINS OF A GIGANTIC CITY, HALF BURIED UNDER SEASHELLS AND MARINE VEGETATION...

FASCINATED, AS THEY PASS, THE TWO MEN LOOK AT THE REMAINS OF A PRODIGIOUS PAST, SPRINGING FROM THE DARK DEEPS LIKE SO MANY GHOSTS...

BUT, AS IT IS MOVING DOWN AN ANCIENT STREET, THE SUBMERSIBLE IS SUDDENLY CAUGHT IN A TERRIFIC EDDY AND FURIOUSLY SHAKEN.

What's happening?

TOSSED ABOUT LIKE A TOY BOAT, THE FRAIL VESSEL SCRAPES THE NOW WOBBLING WALLS; SUDDENLY, ONE OF THEM TILTS OVER AND FALLS ON TOP OF IT...

STUCK BENEATH THE MASSIVE RUBBLE, IT IS IMMOBILISED, AND A WORRIED BLAKE EXCLAIMS FOR THEIR FRIEND'S EAR:

What's going on? We're not moving anymore!

ICARUS'S SLIGHTLY DISTORTED VOICE ANSWERS:

Stay calm... I'll get you out of there... It's obvious that an underwater eruption must be causing all these phenomena!

GLOWING A SINISTER RED THROUGH THE DARK WATERS, A LONG-DORMANT VOLCANO HAS JUST AWAKENED AFTER SEVERAL CENTURIES AND SPEWS OUT ITS BURNING LAVA WITH A THUNDEROUS ROAR.

OUR HEROES' SITUATION IS DIRE, BUT THANKS TO SOME SKILFUL MANOEUVRING BY THE PRINCE, THE BATHYSCAPHE IS FINALLY FREE...

There!!

At last!!!

Good grief! That was close!...

IT IMMEDIATELY RESUMES ITS PROGRESS THROUGH THE CHOPPY SEA AND, ASCENDING RAPIDLY...

... IT SOON SURFACES.

UNBUCKLING IN SECONDS, BLAKE AND MORTIMER DASH TO THE KIOSK, WHICH OPENS RIGHT AWAY.

By Jove! Our sky!

And the good old surface! Hey! What... look over there!...

This place... Heavens, Francis... This is **Sete Cidades**... the Seven Cities' Lake!!!

Could it be!?!... The Seven Cities' Lake, at the bottom of which what we believed to be legend puts the resting place of ancient Atlantis...

BUT, COMING FROM DOWN BELOW, THE PRINCE'S URGENT CALL BRINGS THEM BACK TO REALITY...

Hurry off the boat, my friends!... The command chamber is starting to flood!!

THE SUBMERSIBLE HAVING SAILED NEARER TO THE SHORE, OUR FRIENDS SWIFTLY OBEY...

There!

Hnh!

AS THEY STAND ON THE SHORE, UNCERTAIN OF WHAT TO DO NOW, THEY HEAR THE PRINCE SPEAK TO THEM FOR THE LAST TIME...

Head for the surrounding heights and wait! If, at the ninth hour, nothing has happened, then it will mean that our grand design has failed. And now, for the last time: Farewell!

Adieu, Prince... and good luck!

Farewell, Icarus. God be with you!

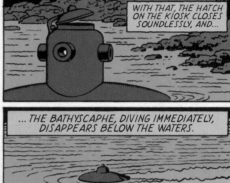

WITH THAT, THE HATCH ON THE KIOSK CLOSES SOUNDLESSLY, AND...

... THE BATHYSCAPHE, DIVING IMMEDIATELY, DISAPPEARS BELOW THE WATERS.

THE TWO COMPANIONS GAZE FOR A MOMENT AT THE VESSEL'S WAKE, THEN, WALKING BRISKLY, START UP THE STEEP PATH THAT OPENS BEFORE THEM.

AFTER A STRENUOUS CLIMB, BLAKE AND MORTIMER HAVE REACHED THE PLACE PRINCE ICARUS POINTED OUT TO THEM. EXHAUSTED, THEY SIT DOWN ON THE GRASS AND SILENTLY OBSERVE THE MYSTERIOUS LAKE THAT STRETCHES AT THEIR FEET, THEIR ONLY COMPANY THE LOW RUMBLING OF THE TITANIC FORCES THAT ARE TURNING THE INSIDE OF THE EARTH UPSIDE DOWN, CAUSING THE GROUND TO SHUDDER...

BUT THEY JUMP TO THEIR FEET AS THE WATER BEGINS CHURNING THREATENINGLY. SUDDENLY, THE WHOLE LAKE LEAPS TO A PRODIGIOUS HEIGHT IN A SINGLE, MASSIVE GEYSER...

... APPEARS SUSPENDED IN THE AIR FOR A SECOND, AND THEN, ALL OF A SUDDEN, FALLS BACK INTO ITS BED AND EMPTIES FROM BELOW WITH HORRIBLE GURGLING SOUNDS...

Good Lord! What's happening?!?...

Atlantis must have collapsed!! They're doomed!!!

61

63

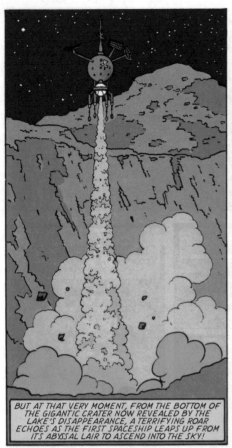

BUT AT THAT VERY MOMENT, FROM THE BOTTOM OF THE GIGANTIC CRATER NOW REVEALED BY THE LAKE'S DISAPPEARANCE, A TERRIFYING ROAR ECHOES AS THE FIRST SPACESHIP LEAPS UP FROM ITS ABYSSAL LAIR TO ASCEND INTO THE SKY!

IT IS THE FLAGSHIP, CARRYING THE BASILEUS HIMSELF WHO, GREAT PILOT OF THE INTERSTELLAR VOID, LEADS HIS PEOPLE INTO SPACE!

Hurray!

Hurray!

THEN, IN LIGHTNING-QUICK SUCCESSION, ALL THE UNITS THAT MAKE UP THIS INCREDIBLE FLEET FOLLOW INTO THE HEAVENS...

AND, WHILE THE ATLANTEANS IN THEIR EXTRAORDINARY MACHINES DISAPPEAR INTO THE DEPTHS OF SPACE, EN ROUTE TOWARDS THEIR NEW DESTINY, BACK ON OUR VENERABLE PLANET TWO MEN ARE TRYING TO BRING THIS FASCINATING STORY TO A CLOSE...

E.P. JACOBS

And so concludes this incredible adventure. And the millenia-old mystery of Atlantis is finally solved!... What will the sceptics say when...

My dear fellow, don't get your hopes up! No one will believe us! They'll just say that we put our personal interpretation on a simple underwater earthquake. They may even accuse us of perpetrating a hoax, or of having had a shared hallucination, or who knows what else!... And, to be fair, how could we hold it against them!?!

THE ADVENTURES OF BLAKE & MORTIMER

1 The Yellow "M"
EDGAR P. JACOBS

2 The Mystery of the Great Pyramid Part 1
EDGAR P. JACOBS

3 The Mystery of the Great Pyramid Part 2
EDGAR P. JACOBS

4 The Francis Blake Affair
VAN HAMME - BENOIT

5 The Strange Encounter
VAN HAMME - BENOIT

6 S.O.S. Meteors
EDGAR P. JACOBS

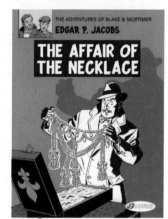

7 The Affair of the Necklace
EDGAR P. JACOBS

8 The Voronov Plot
SENTE - JUILLARD

9 The Sarcophagi of the Sixth Continent Part 1
SENTE - JUILLARD

10 The Sarcophagi of the Sixth Continent Part 2
SENTE - JUILLARD

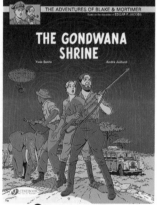

11 The Gondwana Shrine
SENTE - JUILLARD

2012

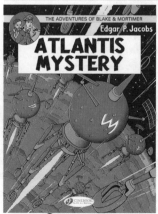

12 Atlantis Mystery
EDGAR P. JACOBS

13 The Curse of the 30 Pieces of Silver Part 1
VAN HAMME - STERNE - DE SPIEGELEER

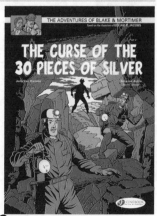

14 The Curse of the 30 Pieces of Silver Part 2
VAN HAMME - AUBIN - SCHRÉDER

WHEN AN ANCIENT CHRISTIAN RELIC SURFACES IN GREECE, BLAKE AND MORTIMER FACE ONE OF THEIR TOUGHEST CHALLENGES EVER.

JEAN VAN HAMME

THE CURSE OF THE 30 PIECES OF SILVER
Part 1

JUNE 2012

PUBLISHED BY

CINEBOOK
The 9th Art Publisher

RENE STERNE   CHANTAL DE SPIEGELEER

THE ADVENTURES OF BLAKE & MORTIMER
Based on the characters of EDGAR P. JACOBS

Part 1

THE CURSE OF THE 30 PIECES OF SILVER

Jean Van Hamme

René Sterne

Chantal De Spiegeleer

9th CINEBOOK
The 9th Art Publisher

Wait, boy. I'm going to get you out of there, don't worry.

WOOFF!
WOOFF!

AFTER GATHERING A HANDFUL OF DRY TWIGS, THE YOUNG SHEPHERD CLIMBS DOWN INTO THE CREVICE...

...AND SLIDES DOWN A FEW FEET ON A SLOPE OF DIRT AND PEBBLES.

HAVING SAFELY REACHED SOLID GROUND, HE LIGHTS HIS IMPROVISED TORCH WITH HIS OLD LIGHTER...

... AND DISCOVERS AN INCREDIBLE SIGHT!

???

What's going on, Triton? Where are you?

WOOOOOOO...
WOOOOOOO...

WOOOOOOOOOOO...

By Saint Dimitrios!?!

You're scared, eh, Triton? Me, too. Don't worry. We'll get out of here.

But first, I'd like to know what's in that casket. There might be something valuable in there.

GRRR...

BUT AS THE YOUNG BOY LIFTS THE LID OF THE METAL CASKET, A STRONG DRAFT SUDDENLY SMOTHERS THE FLAMES OF HIS TORCH.

THE CURSE OF THE 30 PIECES OF SILVER - Part 1

②

TWO WEEKS AND 5,000 MILES LATER, AT THE PENITENTIARY AT JACKSONVILLE, PENNSYLVANIA, ANOTHER EVENT TAKES PLACE—MORE DRAMATIC THAN, IF APPARENTLY UNRELATED TO, THE PREVIOUS ONE.

SLOW

SPEED LIMIT 5

IT'S EXERCISE TIME, AND THE INMATES ARE SPREADING THROUGH THE YARD IN SMALL GROUPS, WATCHED BY HEAVILY ARMED GUARDS.

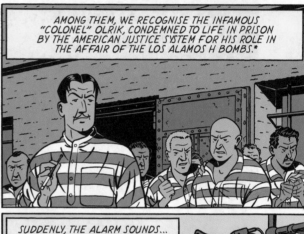

AMONG THEM, WE RECOGNISE THE INFAMOUS "COLONEL" OLRIK, CONDEMNED TO LIFE IN PRISON BY THE AMERICAN JUSTICE SYSTEM FOR HIS ROLE IN THE AFFAIR OF THE LOS ALAMOS H BOMBS.*

SUDDENLY, THE ALARM SOUNDS...

WEEOOEEOOEEOOOO

... FOR THREE COMPLETELY UNMARKED, LOW-FLYING HELICOPTERS ARE APPROACHING THE PRISON.

BEFORE THE GUARDS HAVE A CHANCE TO REACT, TWO OF THE AIRCRAFT OPEN FIRE ON THE GUARD TOWERS...

... WHILE THE THIRD DIVES TOWARDS THE YARD...

? ?! ?? ??

③

*SEE THE STRANGE ENCOUNTER.

THE CURSE OF THE 30 PIECES OF SILVER - Part 1

THE STRANGE ENCOUNTER

Jean Van Hamme   Ted Benoit

Based on the characters of EDGAR P. JACOBS

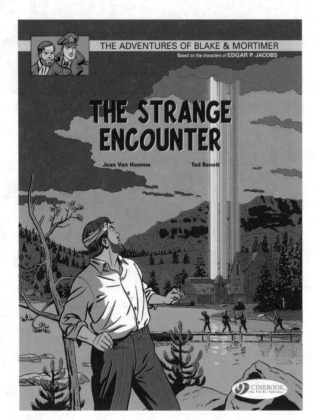

Blake and Mortimer head to the United States to investigate the mysterious circumstances surrounding the discovery of a 177-year-old body, which appears to have died very recently. The body is that of a Scottish major, Mortimer's forebear, who was leading a British military expedition to the US in 1777, where he was swallowed up by a strange multi-coloured light-beam shining down from the sky. Blake and Mortimer fight men in black armed with green-laser guns and soldiers emerging from the past in order to save the Earth from complete obliteration.

Jean **Van Hamme** is one of Belgium's most successful contemporary novelists and comics writers. His most popular successes are "Thorgal" (illustrated by **Rosinski**), "Largo Winch" (illustrated by **Francq**), "Lady S." (illustrated by **Aymond**), translated and published in English by Cinebook, and "XIII" (illustrated by **Vance**). In 2005, he was appointed "Officier des Arts et des Lettres" by the French Minister of Culture.

The artist Ted **Benoit** is a big admirer and supporter of the Clear Line graphic style instituted by **Hergé** and E. P. **Jacobs**. His work is described simply as a combination of extravagance, meticulousness and intelligence. For over 30 years, Ted **Benoit** has been creating work of surprisingly powerful simplicity, from the "Vers la Ligne Claire" collection in 1979 to the "Un Nouveau Monde" collection published in 2006.

AFTER GOING THROUGH PASSPORT CONTROL AND CLAIMING THEIR LUGGAGE, THE TWO FRIENDS GET TO THE AIRPORT'S ARRIVAL HALL. AMONG THE CROWD WAITING FOR THE PASSENGERS FROM LONDON, MORTIMER LOCATES AN ASIAN MAN HOLDING A SIGN WITH HIS NAME.

PROFESSOR P. MORTIMER

Welcome to the United States, Professor Mortimer. I am Jimmy Tcheng, Dr Kaufman's assistant.

A pleasure, Mr Tcheng. And this is my friend, Captain Francis Blake.

BUT BLAKE'S PRESENCE SEEMS TO UPSET THE CHINESE-AMERICAN.

Ah... Doc... Doctor Kaufman didn't mention you'd have company...

Don't worry, Mr Tcheng...

THE TWO FRIENDS SAY THEIR GOODBYES...

A happy coincidence, old fellow, if it allowed us to travel together.

I'm counting on you to keep me apprised of the rest of your astounding story, my dear Philip.

... My presence on this flight with the professor is no more than a coincidence. I'm here to take part in a routine meeting with my colleagues in Washington.

... UNAWARE THAT THEY ARE BEING OBSERVED BY TWO INDIVIDUALS WEARING STRANGE SUNGLASSES.

This is the phone number of the hotel where my friends at the FBI got me a reservation. Don't hesitate to call if you need me, old boy. And give my best to the Martians.

WHILE HIS PARTNER KEEPS AN EYE ON OUR FRIENDS, ONE OF THE MEN HAS SLIPPED INTO A PHONE BOOTH AND DIALLED A MYSTERIOUS NUMBER.

A certain Captain Blake is with him... He mentioned the FBI...

By the Devil! If Blake is here, then it's because he's gotten wind of something. He must be eliminated. Here are my instructions...

I suppose you will be flying to Washington?

Oh, no! Enough flying for me! I'd rather drive there. That way I'll get to enjoy the scenery. Have a nice day, Mr Tcheng!

BUT AS THE SINO-AMERICAN LEADS MORTIMER TOWARDS THE DOMESTIC FLIGHT GATES, A STENTORIAN VOICE STOPS THEM IN THEIR TRACKS.

Come on, Professor, we have just enough time to catch the flight to Topeka...

?

PROFESSOR MORTIMER!

⑤

THE STRANGE ENCOUNTER

Edgard Félix Pierre Jacobs (1904–1987), better known under his pen name Edgar P. Jacobs, was a comic book creator (writer and artist), born in Brussels, Belgium. It has been said of Jacobs that he didn't remember a time when he hadn't drawn.

Jacobs assisted fellow Belgian Hergé (Georges Prosper Remi) in the recasting of Hergé's *Tintin in the Congo*, *Tintin in America*, *King Ottokar's Sceptre* and *The Blue Lotus* for book publication. He also contributed directly to both the drawing and storylines for the Tintin double-albums *The Secret of the Unicorn/Red Rackham's Treasure* and *The Seven Crystal Balls/Prisoners of the Sun*.

When the comics magazine *Tintin* was launched on 26th September 1946, it included Jacobs' story *Le secret de l'Espadon* (*The Secret of the Swordfish*). This story would be the first in the Blake and Mortimer series.

The characters of Captain Francis Blake, dashing head of MI5, his friend Professor Philip Mortimer, a nuclear physicist, and their sworn enemy Colonel Olrik became legendary heroes of the 9th art in the long-running series.

After Jacobs' death in 1987, Bob de Moor completed his unfinished last story. In the mid-1990s, the series was continued by the Jacobs Studios with two teams of writers and artists: Van Hamme/Benoit and Sente/Juillard.

		ORIGINAL FRENCH EDITION
1	1950	Le Secret de l'Espadon, T1
2	1953	Le Secret de l'Espadon, T2
3	1953	Le Secret de l'Espadon, T3
4	1954	Le Mystère de la Grande Pyramide, T1
5	1955	Le Mystère de la Grande Pyramide, T2
6	1956	La Marque Jaune
7	1957	L'Énigme de l'Atlantide
8	1959	S.O.S. Météores
9	1962	Le Piège diabolique
10	1967	L'Affaire du Collier
11	1971	Les trois Formules du Professeur Satō, T1
12	1990	Les trois Formules du Professeur Satō, T2 (Jacobs/De Moor)
13	1996	L'Affaire Francis Blake (Van Hamme/Benoit)
14	2000	La Machination Voronov (Sente/Juillard)
15	2001	L'Étrange Rendez-Vous (Van Hamme/Benoit)
16	2003	Les Sarcophages du Sixième Continent, T1 (Sente/Juillard)
17	2004	Les Sarcophages du Sixième Continent, T2 (Sente/Juillard)
18	2008	Le sanctuaire du Gondwana (Sente/Juillard)
19	2009	La malédiction des 30 deniers, T1 (Van Hamme/Sterne/De Spiegeleer)
20	2010	La malédiction des 30 deniers, T2 (Van Hamme/Aubin)

		CINEBOOK EDITION
		The Secret of the Swordfish, Part 1
		The Secret of the Swordfish, Part 2
		The Secret of the Swordfish, Part 3
2	2007	The Mystery of the Great Pyramid, Part 1
3	2008	The Mystery of the Great Pyramid, Part 2
1	2007	The Yellow "M"
12	2012	Atlantis Mystery
6	2009	S.O.S. Meteors
		The Time Trap
7	2010	The Affair of the Necklace
		Professor Satō's Three Formulas, Part 1
		Professor Satō's Three Formulas, Part 2
4	2008	The Francis Blake Affair
8	2010	The Voronov Plot
5	2009	The Strange Encounter
9	2011	The Sarcophagi of the Sixth Continent, Part 1
10	2011	The Sarcophagi of the Sixth Continent, Part 2
11	2011	The Gondwana Shrine
13	2012	The Curse of the 30 Pieces of Silver, Part 1
14	2012	The Curse of the 30 Pieces of Silver, Part 2